The Pot Thief
Who Studied
D. H. Lawrence

J. Michael Orenduff

Aakenbaaken & Kent   New York

Aakenbaaken & Kent

The Pot Thief Who Studied D. H. Lawrence

Aakenbaaken & Kent   67 East 11th Street #625   New York, NY 10003
akeditor@inbox.com

Cover photograph of the D. H. Lawrence Memorial by Mark Linamood, all rights reserved. Mr. Lindamood was a student of Lawrence scholar Dr. Michael Squires of Virginia Tech.

ISBN 978-1-93843-604-8

Acknowledgements

A common topic among mystery fans is whether series should be read in order. *The Pot Thief Who Studied D. H. Lawrence* presents a twist on that question – whether series *can* be read in order. For although *Lawrence* is the 5th *Pot Thief* book to be published, it was the 3rd to be written.

The explanation for this anomaly is simple. I wrote the first draft of *Lawrence* in the spring of 2009. Then I went to Italy for the summer because my wife was scheduled to teach art history in Florence (what better place?). I forgot to take the *Lawrence* manuscript, so I started a new book. *The Pot Thief Who Studied Einstein* was written in front of a window overlooking the *Ponte Vecchio*. With no distractions other than the view, *Einstein* practically wrote itself. So when we returned in the fall, I sent it to the publisher rather than *Lawrence* which needed more work. Thus, *Einstein* became the 3rd in the series after *Pythagoras* and *Ptolemy*. Then *Lawrence* got pushed back again because I decided to write a book set in Santa Fe so that its launch could occur during the Left Coast Crime conference scheduled in that city. Because Santa Fe is a restaurant town, I made it *The Pot Thief Who Studied Escoffier*. Having the launch during the conference turned out to be more of a distraction than a benefit. However, *Einstein* won the Lefty Award at LCC, and I might not have been there had I not written *Escoffier*.

Meanwhile, the *Lawrence* manuscript had not aged well. The characters in any 5th book of a series should incorporate in their attitudes, actions and dialogue the events they experienced in the first four books. But the Hubie and Susannah of the *Lawrence* manuscript didn't know about their own adventures in *Einstein* and *Escoffier*. They were in a time warp. I kept the plot and the new characters and rewrote it from the beginning. So *Lawrence* is the 3rd book written but the 5th published and – perhaps most importantly – the 5th in the sense of the development of the characters.

In fact, the roots of this book go back to a visit to the Lawrence Ranch in 1968 while I was a student at the University of New Mexico and another visit to Taos thirty years later. My wife and I were staying at the La Fonda. When the manager learned she is an art historian, he asked if she would like to see some paintings by D. H. Lawrence. He unlocked a room in the back and allowed us to see about ten paintings, all signed by Lawrence. It felt like being in a privileged place. This event sparked my interest in Lawrence's connection with Taos

Thanks to Lisa Airey, Andy Anderson, Carolyn Anderson, Linda Aycock, Claire Orenduff Bartos, Marina DiPilato, Mary Fairchild, Kate Feuille, Ofélia Nikolova, Jane Robinson and Dee Suchil who read various drafts at various times. I know this list is not complete, for which I apologize, but the reading has been taking place on and off for three years.

Thanks to Donna Fletcher Crow for providing Miss Gladys with the cookie salad recipe.

The Lawrence Ranch Conference Center in this book is fictional. All other references to the ranch and the historical personages associated with it are accurate to the best of my knowledge. None of the characters in the plot are real, nor are any of them based on any employees of the University of New Mexico.

I owe much to Art Bachrach who gave generously of his time and knowledge to help me integrate D. H. Lawrence into the story. Now that Art is gone, my trips to Taos will never be quite the same.

Dedication

To Art Bachrach (1923-2011),
scientist, scholar, author, bookseller and friend.

1

Opportunity didn't bother to knock. It just walked into my shop in the guise of a man with a broad face and pronounced epicanthic eye folds.

Of course I didn't recognize him as opportunity. Nor did I think he was a customer. In the twenty years I've been in business, I've never had an Indian buy a pot.

He made no eye contact as he turned to the first piece of merchandise, an ancient *olla* from Santo Domingo. He studied it for perhaps thirty seconds. His movement to the next pot was so contained it seemed as though he was still and I was the one moving. Like when a boat moves away from a dock, something I never experience in Albuquerque.

I watched him survey the merchandise in this fashion for a few minutes then went back to *The Wooing of Malkatoon* by Lew Wallace, a book so bad I couldn't put it down.

When my visitor finally approached the counter, I marked my place in the book and studied him. The heavy-lidded eyes looked weary, his face impassive. His sparse facial hair was unshaven. His worn jeans and stained chambray shirt gave him the look of someone who might ask you for spare change.

And yet... there was another layer, a sort of *pentimento*. What could be read as resignation might also be strength. Someone comfortable enough in his skin that he feels no need to demonstrate it to others. Did his countenance reflect five hundred years of white dominance or five centuries of quiet resistance?

He stopped four feet from me. His hooded eyes seemed to take in the entire room without focusing on anything specific.

"You don't have any pots from my people."

His sibilant words drifted across my eardrums like tumbleweeds over dry sand.

"Picuris?"

"Taos," he said. "How you know?"

He probably counted Picuris as a correct answer because Taos and Picuris are the only two places that speak the northern *Tiwa* language. I thought I heard the accent. The southern version is spoken in the two pueblos closest to Albuquerque - Sandia and Isleta. A variety of *Tiwa* was also spoken in Texas, where it was spelled *Tigua*. The pueblo there – also on the Rio Grande – was named like the one near Albuquerque but spelled with a 'Y' in the little village of Ysleta, long ago swallowed up by the El Paso metropolis.

But my fascination with Taos stems not from their language but from their traditional pottery. It was unlike any produced in the other pueblos of New Mexico. Their utilitarian style made Taos pottery less popular with collectors than the elaborate polychrome works of San Juan or the black-on-blacks of San Ildefonso.

The reason I had no pots from Taos wasn't a matter of taste. I specialize in antique pieces, and old pots from Taos are rare because they were often purchased by local Hispanics and Anglos for everyday use which led to their eventually being broken or discarded. Very few people collected them.

When I explained this to my visitor, he nodded.

There was a long silence. I knew to avoid small talk. I looked outside to the deserted sidewalk. Too late in the year for skiers, too early for summer tourists.

"I can get you three Taos pots from the 1920s," he finally said, eyes looking through me.

I told him I was interested.

"First you have to get an old one for me," he said.

The offer to get me three pieces if I got him one seemed odd. I asked how I could get an old Taos pot for him.

He finally looked me in the eyes. "You'll have to steal it."

Maybe he wasn't opportunity personified. Maybe he was temptation.

2

I guess he knew about my reputation. My name is Hubert Schuze and I'm a pot thief. I stole my first pots back in the eighties as a student on a summer dig with the anthropology program at the University of New Mexico. I sold them for enough money to make a down payment on my building in Old Town which has my shop in the front and my residence in the rear.

Except I didn't really steal them. In the first place, they didn't come out of the excavation site. I knew the faculty leaders were digging in the wrong place as soon as I saw them drive the stakes and stretch the string. After studying the ruins and the lay of the land for a week, I dug my own hole away from the dig site and found three rare intact pots.

In the second place, digging up old pots wasn't illegal back then. But that didn't stop the University from kicking me out of school. They hinted I might be reinstated if I returned the pots and apologized. But I didn't know who to apologize to. The potter whose work I unearthed had been dead for a thousand years, and I'm confident she never gave much thought to what would happen to her works a millennium after she made them. I imagine her as the practical sort. If I were to ask her whether I should trade her pots for the right to attend more classes or sell them to get money for a house, she would advise me to take the money and run.

She and I were born under the same desert sky and looked up at the same starscape. We enjoyed the feel of wet clay between our fingers. We shared the disappointment of discovering a fissure when the firing temperature fluctuated too much. Neither of us ever had much interest in living anywhere else.

We are from different tribes. Her people arrived on this continent from the west, mine from the east. But we are both human, and like all members of our species, we need shelter, food, drink, and companionship. We laugh and cry. We feel pain and sorrow, triumph and joy.

I don't know any of the details of her life, but I know she was a potter, and that's enough for me. She could distinguish a well-made pot from an ill-formed one. She took pride in her work. I take pride in mine. I also take pride in the three pots of hers I found. Though I didn't make them, I'm proud to share membership with her in the potters' clan of the human tribe.

When I lay me down to sleep, I sometimes look up at the *vigas* of my ceiling and whisper a silent thanks to her. Which is not the same as an apology. I don't think she would want one. I think she's happy her pots are with someone who appreciates them instead of being hidden in the earth.

The University forgave me a couple of years ago though I never asked them to do so. I was credited with recovering a rare Mogollon pot that had gone missing from their *Valle del Rio* Museum. The recovered pot was auctioned off at a fund-raiser with the understanding it would revert to the Museum, and my filthy-rich attorney matched the donation so that the University ended up with a hefty new scholarship fund.

The fact that I was the one who had extricated the pot from the Museum to begin with was kept tactfully secret by my attorney. And that's as much as I think I should say about that.

I'm not really a thief. I don't break into homes and steal the silverware. I'm a treasure hunter. But treasure hunting, a fun and profitable hobby enjoyed by thousands, was criminalized by the passage of ARPA, the Archaeological Resources Protection Act.

It's a ridiculous law, and I have chosen to disregard it. There are more archaeological resources in the ground than could be excavated in a million years, and only a few of them need protecting. During the aforementioned summer dig, I spent one afternoon idly sifting through the sand at Gran Quivera. I discovered nine perfect arrow heads, sixty-seven broken or chipped arrowheads, and about a thousand pieces of worked flint. According to ARPA, removing even one of those flint pieces would have been a crime.

A crime I did not commit. I admired the work and then left the arrowheads where I found them. I could have sold them, but it would have hardly been worth the effort. Nine arrowheads at the going price back then of a dollar each is nine dollars for four hours work – not even minimum wage.

Pots are another matter. The three I unearthed that summer brought me $25,000. In today's dollars that would be... I don't know. I don't even know why we worry about it. It was $25,000 then and I spent it then, so what difference does it make what it would be now?

3

Of course I didn't explain my treasure hunting background to my visitor. He already knew I was a pot thief, and I doubt he had any interest in knowing why.

He handed me an old cracked black and white photograph of a smiling Indian on a horse holding a shiny pot. Actually, the Indian was holding the shiny pot. The horse couldn't have done so because all four of his feet were on the ground.

"The man on the horse is my great-grandfather. This was taken the day he took that pot to Mr. Lawrence."

"D. H. Lawrence?"

He shrugged. "I don't know his other names. It's the man the ranch is named for."

"Why did your great-grandfather take a pot to Lawrence?"

"Tony Lujan asked him to. It is my people's custom to take a bowl of food to a newcomer."

Tony Lujan was the Taos Indian who married Mabel Dodge, the wealthy heiress who persuaded Lawrence to come to Taos.

I glanced down at the photo again. "This is the pot you want me to steal?"

"White man law might call it that. But it belongs to my great-grandfather. He made it. Now he wants it back."

There were strands of grey in his ponytail and crow's feet around his eyes. He had to be at least forty. Allowing twenty years for each generation, his great-grandfather would have to be pushing the century mark.

"Your great-grandfather is still alive?"

He shook his head.

"He told you he wanted it back before he died?"

Another shake of the head. Another long silence.

Finally, he said, "His spirit asked me to bring the pot home."

I looked down again at the photo. "What was his name?"

"His Spanish name was Fidelio Duran."

"And his Indian name?"

There was a long silence before he answered. "He didn't sign his pots with his Indian name."

I assumed that was his way of saying I didn't need to know his great-grandfather's Indian name. I didn't need to know my visitor's name either, Spanish or Indian. I could find him at the Pueblo just by asking around. But I asked him anyway, and he said his name was Cyril Duran.

"So if I find a pot that looks like this and is signed 'Fidelio Duran', that's the one you want?"

He made one almost imperceptible nod.

"Where would I look for it?"

"I don't know."

"And you'll trade me three Taos pots from the same era, the twenties?"

Another slight nod.

"Made by your great-grandfather?"

"No, his wife."

It took me a couple of seconds to make the connection. My pulse spiked.

"Dulcinea Duran?"

He nodded.

4

After Cyril Duran left, I locked the store and pawed through the drawer where I toss mail and papers I don't know what to do with. I found the invitation from my *alma mater*. They wanted me to come to the Lawrence Ranch to give a presentation on pueblo pottery to a group of university benefactors who would be gathering for a retreat.

I don't like to travel and I don't do presentations. I'd thrown the invitation in the drawer rather than the trash because I thought I might need the stipend they were offering. Now my keeping it seemed serendipitous.

But it was no longer the stipend that interested me. It would be chump change compared to what I might get if I could find the Fidelio Duran pot and trade it for three pots by Dulcinea, the most famous pueblo potter of the early 20th Century. Her fame has now been eclipsed by Maria Martinez of San Ildefonso, but Dulcinea was the first superstar potter.

Dulcinea Duran was a gifted potter even before she was taken under the wings of the wives of the robber barons who came to Taos to take the mountain air and study the aborigines. They told her they would buy her pots if she would use a wheel in order to make them symmetrical. I imagine they even ordered the wheel from back east and had it shipped. It wouldn't surprise me to learn that they had electricity run to the pueblo in order for her to plug it in. Except for the fact that even today, there is neither electricity nor running water in the part of the original pueblo building where she lived. Those structures are used today mostly for ceremonial purposes, new residences having been built at various locations on the hundred thousand acres owned by the Taos Pueblo. Technically, the land is held in trust by the U.S. Government, but in reality it belonged to the Indians for eight hundred years before there even *was* a U. S. Government, and in my mind it still does.

Dulcinea's pots became all the rage and were exhibited widely in Philadelphia, New York, and Boston. The museums didn't actually purchase the pots, no doubt considering them crafts rather than *beaux arts*. They probably showed them merely because the women who owned them were wealthy and influential. The fad eventually waned, and the works were returned from the museums to the 'cottages' in Newport. Finding a genuine Dulcinea today would be like finding a Van Gogh.

I stared at the invitation and wrestled with my conscience.

An industrious lad with long hair and an easy smile had entered my shop a week earlier with a rack of greeting cards which he offered to leave on my counter for free. The cards depicted buzzards perched on saguaro cactuses and making witty remarks shown in little bubbles above their heads. I could sell them, he explained earnestly, for any price I chose and pay him after the fact at the bargain price of only fifty cents for each one sold.

He left with the rack still under his arm and, if we are to believe what he said, utter disbelief that I would decline the opportunity to make money with no investment. I like to make money. But I love my pristine shop and simple life even more. I do not sell postcards or candy. I have no vending machines. I'm not in the trinket business.

One result of this Spartan approach is I am not overrun with customers, and I often have cash-flow problems. It is a painful admission because – speaking of painful admissions – I graduated with a degree in accounting. My graduate work was in anthropology until I got booted, but as an undergraduate, I started as a math major. I switched to accounting because everyone told me that's where the jobs were. It was the only conventional decision I ever made, and I learned my lesson.

When I make a $15,000 sale, I live off it until it is gone. When I make a really big sale, I give some of it away because I don't like having a lot of money all at once. My father was fond of saying that money is like manure. It's good to spread it around, but if you leave it in one big pile it stinks.

I know what you're thinking – how can you get in line for the money I give away? It's a short line. I partially support my nephew Tristan, I pay the medical bills for my former nanny Consuela, and I donate to a scholarship fund for kids from the pueblo where I volunteered back in my undergraduate days.

For the past few months, Tristan had been forced to live off his part-time earnings and the scholarship fund was depleted. Consuela Sanchez' kidney problems were worsening and her medical bills soaring. Now a transplant loomed. I had done the paperwork to apply for assistance which Consuela and Emilio qualified for, but even with that, the "patient responsibility" portion came to $46,000, half of which they wanted in advance.

Just one of the Dulcinea pots would cover that. The debate with my conscience was going well until it actually spoke. What it said was that if Consuela's transplant expense justified stealing the Fidelio Duran pot, then it also justified robbing a bank.

Don't you just hate it when your conscience is right?

I'm not a thief. I needed to know I would not be stealing the pot. Cyril said the pot belonged to his great-grandfather. Why not just take his word for it? But he also said white man law might call it stealing. Why worry about that? Surely he knew more about his great-grandfather than he did about the law.

Mr. Conscience vetoed that one as too obviously a rationalization. He's a smug little devil.

I needed to think harder. I asked myself what was the real issue. Who owns the pot? Who deserves the pot? Who should decide? What time is it?

The last question was the only one I could answer. It was well past five, and I was thirsty.

5

It was a dark and stormy night.

I'm not kidding. It really was.

Which was unusual. Not the dark part. Nights are always dark except above the Arctic Circle in summer. And maybe below the Antarctic Circle in summer; I'm not certain about that. But the rain part was unusual. Evening rain is as rare in Albuquerque as English ivy. Our rain is almost always in the form of afternoon showers.

I was at my usual watering hole, *Dos Hermanas Tortilleria*. Martin Seepu was standing in the rain staring up at the sky. I knew why because I had seen him do it before.

Susannah was more sensibly ensconced under the veranda.

I licked the final grains of salt from the rim of my first margarita. A few more and I could silence Mr. Conscience, at least for the evening.

Susannah waits tables at *La Placita* in Old Town and takes evening classes at the University. There was a time when she was a full-time day student, but she began to feel guilty about taking her parents' money and not making progress towards a degree, so she took up waitressing and switched to night classes. She's majored in pre-vet, pre-dental, and pre-law. When she ran out of pre- majors, she did sociology, psychology, and maybe a few other ologies I've forgotten. Currently she's in art history.

Martin once told me that standing under the stars makes him feel serene. I don't know how standing out in the rain made him feel. Wet, I suppose.

"Why is he standing in the rain?" Susannah asked.

"It's an Indian thing," I answered.

"It's not an Indian thing," he yelled over the drumbeat of raindrops on the corrugated tin roof of the veranda, "anyone can learn to do it."

"Do what?" Susannah asked.

"Tell how long it will rain," I said.

Martin joined us at the table, shaking his head vigorously and spraying us like a dog. "You stare up through the rain until your eyes focus on the drops farthest away from you, the ones that appear to be the smallest. Then you gauge how far the smallest drops are above the largest ones."

"And?" asked Susannah.

"If the small ones seem to be real high, it's a passing storm. If they're low, they're coming from low-level clouds, and the rain will last longer."

"You're kidding, right?"

He took a sip of his Tecate. "This one's going to stop in about an hour."

"You're soaking wet," she observed needlessly.

"Why do you pale-faces avoid rain? Being in the rain is just as natural as being in the dry air. It won't shrink you."

"Which is a good thing in your case," I said. Martin is 5' 6".

"You're the same height as me, *Kemo Sabe*."

"True, but I used to be six feet tall before I spent too much time in the rain."

I sipped my margarita and listened to Martin explain his tribe's meteorological techniques. No mechanical wind gauges, no Doppler radar and no weather satellites, but he gets it right more often than the television weather man. I should have paid attention when he told me there was going to be one more big snow before summer, but I wasn't worried about the weather.

I was preoccupied with the Fidelio Duran pot. I didn't tell them about that, but I did tell them about the invitation to the D. H. Lawrence Ranch.

"D. H. Lawrence?" asked Susannah. "As in the painter?"

"There's a painter named D. H. Lawrence?"

"Yeah. He's not famous like Georgia O'Keeffe and some of the others who worked here. In fact, I'd never heard of him until we had a lecture on the painters of New Mexico earlier this semester. They included a few of his works in the lecture, so I guess he's not a total unknown."

I was speculating on the odds of a painter and a writer both being named D. H. Lawrence and both working in New Mexico. I figured they were long. "You sure he isn't the writer?"

"I saw his paintings, Hubie. He's a painter."

"What did they look like?"

"Not that great to tell the truth. I could see why he isn't that famous."

"But what did they look like?"

"All the ones they showed were nudes in suggestive poses. He used broad brush strokes and curvy renderings like *The Scream* by Munch."

"Nudes in suggestive poses are probably what Lawrence would do. It has to be the same guy. I didn't know he painted."

"I didn't know he wrote. Did he write anything I would have heard of?"

I stared at her. "*Lady Chatterley's Lover?*"

"I think I've heard of that," she said casually.

I was about to make a caustic remark about America's public schools when it came to me that the court decision overturning the ban on *Lady Chatterley's Lover* was not only before Susannah was born, it was even before I was born.

So I told her about the book's lurid reputation and the Supreme Court's extension of free speech to cover sexually explicit literature. She asked if I had ever read the book. I invoked my right against self-incrimination and refused to answer.

"So they named a ranch after him?" she asked.

"I'm not sure. Maybe it was his ranch. I think he and his wife had it back in the twenties or thirties. Lawrence died a long time ago, but his wife lived on the ranch for many years. She willed it to the University when she died."

"It must be swanky if they use it to entertain dignitaries."

"I don't know. I've never been there. But now I have the chance, and I don't know whether to take it."

"It sounds like fun to me. Probably a lot of good food and drink. And the Taos area is beautiful."

"They want me do something involving pots, and I'm not sure how that would entertain dignitaries."

"Everybody likes hearing about the Anasazi. Just take some of your old pots up there and do a show and tell."

"I don't like taking pots out of my shop because they might get broken."

She shrugged. "Then just take some of your fakes."

"Maybe," I replied and turned to Martin.

He was one of the pueblo kids I tutored in my undergraduate days. His uncle is a potter. "Maybe your uncle could come with me."

"He doesn't like white people."

"He likes me."

"No he doesn't."

"What if I offered to pay him?"

"Cash or beads?"

"Cash. They're offering me a big stipend, so I'd be in a sharing mood."

"What would he have to do?"

"Maybe talk about the traditional designs on his pots?"

"He's not much of a talker."

"I've noticed. Maybe he could just dress up in a feathered headdress and look fierce."

"I look fiercer than he does. Maybe I could do it."

"You don't know anything about pots."

"True, but the dignitaries wouldn't know that."

Martin does look fierce if you don't know him. He weighs about 170, all of it muscle, and he has a wide face with a strong chin and dark penetrating eyes. He's actually a pussy cat, but the impassive expression he wears masks it as effectively as would an application of war paint.

Susannah asked him why he hadn't learned about pots growing up around his uncle.

"My mother said it's better to work with your mind than your hands."

"Mine, too," said Susannah. "That's why I've been in college so long."

"You told me you're in college to meet a man," I reminded her.

"That's working with your mind," she said.

Martin and I glanced at each other.

"Don't go there," she warned, and we didn't.

"Can we get back to whether I should accept the offer to do something at the Ranch?"

"Can we assume these dignitaries are rich?" asked Susannah.

"Since the event is being sponsored by the fund-raising office, I think that's a safe assumption."

"Maybe you could auction off a pot to them."

Martin and I just stared at her.

"Well?" she said defensively, "it's not such a dumb idea. Rich people like to buy expensive and exotic things. You should hear some of the stories we're told in class about art collectors. You never see an Anasazi pot offered as a blue-light special, so why not give them the idea they're getting the chance to buy something no ordinary working stiff can even see, much less buy?"

Martin thought it would be tacky to convert my presentation to a live version of the Shopping Channel. I agreed, but I didn't think it mattered whether Martin and I thought it was classless. What mattered was what the dignitaries thought. The more I considered it, the more I began to think Susannah might be right.

"You're forgetting one small detail," said Martin. "Selling old pots is no longer legal."

"They probably wouldn't know that," said Susannah, "and even if they did, they probably wouldn't care. In fact, it might make having the pot even more desirable."

"Huh?" said Martin.

"She's right," I said. "Some rich collectors specialize in stolen art because it's even rarer than regular art."

"White people are weird," said Martin. I didn't argue the point.

"About ten years ago," said Susannah, "thieves broke into the Gardner Museum in Boston and stole paintings worth three hundred million. Not one of those paintings was ever recovered, and the thieves never sought a ransom, so you have to assume they're in someone's private collection."

"Three hundred million!" said Martin. "That's a lot of *wampum*. Didn't they have guards?"

"It was a guard that let them in."

"Oh, an inside job."

"No," said Susannah, laughing, "the guard wasn't in on it. He admitted later that he was frequently stoned on the job." She shook her head. "They took paintings by Degas, Manet, Vermeer, and Rembrandt. In fact, the Rembrandt they took was the only landscape he ever did."

I sat there wondering if the Archaeological Resources Protection Act covered a three-hundred-year-old Rembrandt landscape. Probably not.

6

Susannah drove to class and Martin returned to his pueblo. I pulled my windbreaker up over my head to keep dry and went home.

Almost. I stopped short of my door, looked around to be certain no one was watching, lowered the windbreaker, and stared up into the rain. I couldn't see anything because I blinked every time a raindrop hit my eye. But I kept at it and eventually overcame the blink reaction by telling myself it was no different from getting water in your eyes when you go swimming.

Which makes sense except for the fact that I don't know how to swim. Living in the desert, swimming never seemed a useful skill to acquire.

Even with my eyes wide open, I could scarcely pick out individual drops, much less tell what size they were. Then it stopped raining. I looked at my watch. It was fifty-five minutes after Martin had said the rain would stop in an hour. I wondered if I could learn to do that. Then realized it was like swimming, a skill rarely needed in New Mexico. Then I wondered why I was standing outside, cold and wet.

I stepped inside and turned to close the door only to see Miss Gladys Claiborne's fringed yellow umbrella coming down the street, presumably with Miss Gladys beneath it. She is, I believe, the only person in Albuquerque who owns an umbrella. In the hand not grasping the umbrella, she held a bag I suspected was full of food.

"Mr. Claiborne always used to talk about people who didn't come in out of the rain," she said, laughing, "but until I saw you tonight, I thought that was just an expression."

"It is an expression, Miss Gladys, and I believe the proper phrasing is 'people who don't have *sense* enough to come in out of the rain'."

She blushed. "I didn't want to say that because it didn't sound polite. Besides, I know for a fact that you are a sensible young man. Now, you go change out of those wet clothes and come back in here and have some of this beef consommé."

Miss Gladys bears the titles of Episcopal Stalwart, Casserole Queen, and proprietor of the eponymous Miss Gladys's Gift Shop located in the west end of my building. Actually, it isn't my building. I own only the east third of it.

I also rent, with an option to buy, the middle third where I sell replicas of Native American pottery. What, you may be wondering, is the difference between a fake and a replica? Simple – a replica is a fake the customer knows is a fake.

Before I took over the middle portion of the building, it housed a gelato parlor. It came onto the market when its proprietor went to prison for murder. I don't want to give you the wrong impression about Old Town. It's actually a safe and pleasant neighborhood. Hundreds of thousands of tourists enjoy visiting here every year, and the only crime they are subjected to is the prices in some of the shops.

I don't think Miss Gladys depends on the income from her shop. How much money can you make in New Mexico selling things like antimacassars? She and her tubercular husband moved to Albuquerque from East Texas many years ago, and he left her well off when he died.

Two things seem higher on her priority list than making money. One is keeping me well fed, and the other is getting me married. In my darker moments I fantasize about buying her out and owning the entire building, but I always feel guilty about that scheme. And don't have enough money to do it.

I'm an only child born late to my parents, a father who was a professor and a mother whose goal in life was to bring gentility to what she considered a rough territory, not an entirely inappropriate characterization when you consider that New Mexico had been a state for only twenty-five years when she moved here as a twenty-year-old bride. Her efforts left no time for cooking and cleaning, so when I was born to her in her early forties, my father hired a *criada*. Consuela Saenz raised me on Mexican food and later taught me to cook it. Her efforts molded my palate to chiles, cilantro, cumin, and lime, and I've never developed a taste for other flavors.

Miss Gladys' cooking normally involves the use of prepared food as ingredients. Campbell's soup and processed cheeses are her staples. But the beef consommé was delicious and I told her so.

"It's the fresh juniper berries," she confided. "Mr. Claiborne always liked my beef consommé, but after we moved out here and were able to get fresh juniper berries, he wanted it every day. I think maybe it soothed the ravages of his disease."

I didn't doubt it. Juniper is one of the commonest plants in New Mexico. Native Americans used its dark blue berries not only as a spice, but as a basic food and also as a medicine for respiratory diseases.

"Miss Gladys," I said between spoonfuls, "what do you know about D. H. Lawrence?"

She blushed again. "My heavens, I barely know what to say. His books were banned by our board of education in Texas."

"Did you ever read anything by him?"

She stared down at her shoes. "I don't believe that's a proper question to ask a lady."

I continued to consume the consommé.

"There was a copy of *Lady Chatterley's Lover* at the public library," she finally said, looking down at the floor. "The library was run by a Yankee lady who simply would not countenance censorship. People in town considered her a free thinker, but I have to admit that I liked her independent spirit."

She looked up, but when my light brown eyes met her sparkling blue ones, she glanced back down. "I tried to read the thing," she said hesitatingly. "I hope you won't think ill of me. I was curious."

"And what did you think of it," I asked.

"I didn't get very far. I couldn't understand a word of it. I suppose I was too simple to understand why it was so nasty."

She took a deep breath as if a weight had been lifted. I finished the soup and placed the spoon in the bowl.

"When I was a boy, I found a copy of that book at Duran Central Pharmacy. I hid behind the bookrack and read the pages that were dog-eared. I was hoping for something prurient, but I didn't understand it either."

"It must have been some pharmacy to sell books like that."

"It wasn't just a pharmacy. It was also a café. Still is, but the Duran who runs it now isn't related to the one who ran it when I was growing up. Maybe the new guy bought it because he wouldn't have to change the sign. Anyway, it used to have one of those lazy-Susan bookracks. But I didn't go there to read. I went there to eat. I'd sit at the lunch counter and eat their chile cheeseburgers smothered with homemade green sauce."

I knew that both of the Durans who ran the pharmacy were Hispanic, and neither had any relationship to Fidelio Duran, but the coincidence of the names added to the peculiar feeling about the timing of the invitation to the Ranch. I was lost in that thought for a moment and then looked up at Miss Gladys. "Their red and green sauces were wonderful, but I'd wager they never made anything as good as this consommé."

She looked at me with a twinkle in her eyes. "I'll leave you this dessert for later, Mr. Schuze. It's called cookie salad, and the recipe comes from Chantelle Blackburn."

A fitting name for one of Miss Gladys's friends, I thought, as she described the concoction. "It's as simple as falling off a log. One small box of instant vanilla pudding mix, 1 cup buttermilk, two 8-ounce containers of frozen whipped topping, two 8-ounce cans of mandarin oranges – drained of course – and one package of fudge-striped cookies crushed into chunks."

Yum.

After Miss Gladys left, I locked up for the night, opened a cold bottle of New Mexico's finest champagne and settled down with Miss Gladys' cookie salad.

You may be perplexed by the phrase, "New Mexico's finest champagne."

I admit our state seems an odd venue for champagne production, but then the grapes are grown in the southern part of the state near Truth or Consequences, which is a strange venue for just about anything other than a meeting of the Odd Place Names Society.

After one bite of the cookie salad, I decided the Gruet *Blanc de Noir* deserved better. I'm sure it was a delightful dessert immediately after Miss Gladys assembled it, but it hadn't worn well. The dressing had turned the crumbled cookies to a soggy mess. Fortunately, I had an excellent substitute on hand – chocolate with Mexican *canela* and red *chile* from Chimayo. It's made here in Albuquerque by an artisanal chocolate kitchen called Cocopotamus.

As the owner of a pottery shop called Sprits in Clay, I guess I shouldn't complain about a cutesy name. Because of the *canela* and *chile*, I think a Spanish word would be better, but by any name the stuff is addictive.

I spent the remainder of the evening eating too much chocolate, drinking too much champagne and thinking too much about Fidelio Duran, Dulcinea Duran, the Duran Pharmacy and David Herbert Lawrence.

7

The next day at five, I was back at *Dos Hermanas* for my regular rendezvous with Susannah, an appointment we keep with almost religious fervor. It serves as a relaxing transition for her between work and class, and it gives me someone to talk to after spending most days with little human contact.

We talk about old movies, her studies, my illegal capers, her quest for True Romance, and anything else one of us finds of interest. She's more than just someone to talk to – she's my partner in crime. In her late twenties with all the enthusiasm and energy of youth, she's fresh, irreverent, inquisitive and funny. Despite those attributes and being attractive in a girl-next-door sort of way, her love life is rockier than a trout stream.

We don't have that much in common. She's two decades younger, grew up on a ranch and likes sports. I grew up in the city and don't know a hat trick from a home run. Maybe our differences are the key to our friendship.

Dos Hermanas has tables both inside and on the veranda. A chill in the air drove us to our favorite inside table against the north wall. After Angie brought our first round, I told Susannah about Cyril Duran.

"Why didn't you tell me about it last night? This changes the whole conversation about you going to the Lawrence Ranch."

"Sorry, Suze, but it's embarrassing to admit that a perfect stranger walks into your shop and asks you to steal something. Of course, that's what Carl Wilkes did when I got mixed up with the *Valle del Rio* Museum."

She smiled at the mention of the museum caper. "Remember when I kicked in the door of Berdal's apartment?"

"How could I forget it? O.K., you're right. I should have told you. I know I'll need your help again."

"What do you need me to do?"

"How about help me figure out where to look for the pot?"

"Maybe it's in a display case right in the Conference Center where you'll be staying."

"I hope it's buried in the ground. That way I won't feel so much like a thief if I take it."

"Do you even know what it looks like?"

I handed her the photograph. "The guy in the picture is Duran's great-grandfather. He made the pot. The picture was taken as he was about to take it to Lawrence."

"Did Lawrence collect pueblo pottery?"

"I have no idea. I know it's a longshot, but I'd love to find that pot."

She gave me that mischievous smile. "What about your claim that you're not a thief?"

The thief debate is a staple of our repartee. "You know my logic, Suze. Pots in the ground don't belong to anyone, so—"

"I know. They belong to whoever finds them. But despite your wish to the contrary, this pot isn't likely to be in the ground. It belongs to someone. Maybe Lawrence's estate or the University."

"Duran says it belongs to his great-grandfather who wants it back."

"His great-grandfather is still alive?"

"No, he died long before Cyril was born."

"I don't get it?"

"His great-grandfather's spirit told Cyril to bring the pot back home."

"You buy that, Hubie?"

"I'm skeptical but open-minded."

I could see the wheels turning as she ran her finger around the rim of her saltless glass. "It's too much of a coincidence."

"What is?"

"First, you get invited to the Lawrence Ranch. Then right after that, this Duran character asks you steal a pot from the same place."

"It wasn't right after. It was a week or so."

She had swung into her mystery mode.

"Remember when you took that blindfolded ride to appraise a pot collection? Except the guy didn't really want an appraisal. He wanted you there because you're a pot thief, and he wanted to frame you for the theft of the pots he stole."

I shuddered remembering it.

"You know why you never see these things coming, Hubert? It's because you don't read murder mysteries. There are no coincidences. Duran first had to get you invited to the Ranch. Then he had to entice you to accept the invitation by feeding you that cockamamie story about his great-grandfather. He probably already has the pot, but the people at the Ranch haven't noticed it missing. So after you return empty-handed because you can't find the pot, Duran will tip the cops, and you'll take the fall."

I shook my head and took a gulp of my drink, selecting a part of the rim laden with salt. "No way. The pot belongs to his great-grandfather. He gave me that picture of him holding it. He just needs me to retrieve it."

She shook her head at my gullibility and held the photo up towards me.

"Does the guy on the horse look like Duran?"

"Well, it's an old picture and cracked, and—"

"This could be a picture of anyone. And when you're arrested and tell the police you went there looking for the pot because Duran's great-grandfather's spirit told you to, they'll just laugh at you."

She studied the photo for a moment. "You know what? You might have caught a break this time. Was Duran wearing gloves when he came to your shop?"

"Indians don't wear gloves," I said dismissively.

"They do in Cleveland," she said unaccountably. Then she laughed. I don't know why.

She wagged the photo over the table. "His fingerprints are on here. That proves it came from him, and he was using it to set you up." She wrapped the photo carefully in some napkins and dropped it into her purse.

"Don't tell me you have a fingerprint kit at home."

"Of course not. I'm just saving it for when you get arrested."

"I'm not going to get arrested," I said with more assurance than I felt. I didn't think Duran would go to all that trouble to frame me for a simple theft, but I had to admit the timing was a worrisome coincidence.

8

I awoke late and famished and prepared two helpings of *huevos rancheros*. I ate one and gave the other to Geronimo, an animal of undetermined ancestry who lives with me. His license says he's a dog, but he looks part anteater.

I washed the dishes, showered and shaved, brushed and flossed, put on a pair of tan chinos and a light blue oxfordcloth button-down shirt and stepped out into the crisp New Mexico morning with Geronimo on a leash.

Then I stepped back inside and put on my windbreaker. The front that arrived after Albuquerque's rare monsoon had dropped the temperature into the twenties. I remembered Martin's prediction about snow, but the sky was bright blue, and the sun's rays pierced the dry air with ease, warming my face as I headed to the library.

I got only as far as the San Felipe de Neri Church on the north side of the Plaza where I saw Father Groaz gazing up at the two bell towers, unlikely structures combining Spanish colonial and Victorian architecture but somehow managing to look just right in the setting.

Father Groaz also looks like he belongs. His craggy face, barrel chest, and bushy beard give him the look of a frontiersman, but as soon as he speaks, a different image comes to mind. Transylvania. He has a deep voice and an Eastern European accent that sounds like something out of an old Hollywood movie about vampires or werewolves.

"Gud marnik, Youbird," he said without looking down.

"Good morning, Father. What are you looking at?"

"I wass just enjoying the sun while I wait for the police," he said, "but mebbe I should be seeking help from aboff to find out who stole the paintings."

It took me just a moment to remember that Father Groaz had not been with Martin and me when Susannah was telling us about the stolen paintings from the Gardner Museum.

"What paintings are those?"

"The ones in the parish hall. And the worst thing is, Youbird, they do not belong to us. They were vary kindly loaned to us by a famous artist."

I knew the paintings he was referring to. The Church had been observing the tricentennial of the laying of its cornerstone in the early 1700s, and several of the events in the year-long celebration focused on Native American culture since Neri had originally been a missionary church to the local pueblos.

Father Groaz was a parish priest in Taos before coming to St. Neri. In between he was in the Jemez Valley at the home for wayward priests. The place has a more circumspect name, but I can't remember it. He was not wayward. He was on the staff.

I'm not Catholic, but I consider Father Groaz my spiritual advisor. He also provided assistance of a more secular nature when I was falsely accused of murder. The police thought the victim had attempted to scribble my name, but the writing turned out to be in the Cyrillic alphabet. Groas' native tongue uses that bizarre script with its backwards 'R', a letter that looks like the number 3 and other oddities. He not only explained the meaning of the note the victim left, he gave me the complete history of Cyrillic to add to my already vast store of useless knowledge.

Jaune Quick-To-See Smith had allowed the Church to display some of her artwork, and Susannah and I had attended her lecture at the opening of the show in the parish hall.

Father Groaz took me inside the locked parish hall where I looked at the blank wall where her paintings had been. I was commiserating with the good father when Detective Whit Fletcher arrived with a pair of crime-scene techs.

"Good morning, Father," said Fletcher. "These boys here are Juan and Alan. They're CSI guys like you see on television. Say hello to Father Groaz, boys."

The two young techs, obviously used to Fletcher's manner, smiled and nodded at the big priest.

"And this here," Fletcher said, tilting his head in my direction, "is Hubert Schuze. We can rule him out as a suspect 'cause he don't steal paintings. He steals pots."

The tech guys smiled and nodded again as if Fletcher were kidding me. Fletcher and I have done a few deals over the years. He's been helpful to me when I was mistakenly charged with murder. One thing he knows about me – in addition to the fact that I dig up old pots – is I am definitely not capable of murder. One thing I know about him is he likes to make money on the side when it doesn't get in the way of solving a major crime. He trusts me to keep quiet about his supplemental income, and I trust him to help me out with police matters.

Father Groaz told Fletcher he was sure the paintings were on the wall last night when he locked up after catechism class. He had gone in that morning to straighten up and discovered they were gone.

"Who was the artist?" asked Fletcher

"Jaune Smith," answered Groaz.

"John Smith? Sounds more like an alias than an artist."

"It's not 'John'," I said, "it's 'Jaune'. She's a woman."

He took out a notebook and told me to spell it, and I said, "W-o-m-a-n."

The techs laughed but immediately stopped when Fletcher shot them a look. Then I spelled her name, explaining that her middle name was 'Quick-To-See' and was hyphenated with all three words capitalized.

"What the hell kind of name is that?"

"She's Native American," I said.

"I never heard of any Indians around here having a name like that."

"She's not from here originally. She lives over in Corrales, but she was raised on the Flathead Reservation in Montana."

"You know her, Hubert?"

"No, but I know of her. She's a very famous artist, Whit."

"Is that a fact," he said. It was just an expression, not a question.

9

Geronimo and I took our leave to pursue my original destination, the Special Collections Branch of the Albuquerque Public Library on the corner of Central and Edith. It's a beautiful old adobe building with organic shapes and the traditional New Mexico palette of sand-colored stucco and turquoise-painted doors and window trim.

I started to tie Geronimo to a utility pole on the corner, but he tugged me over to a bench in the sun by the south wall. I tied the lead to the bench upon which he immediately curled up and went to sleep.

The Special Collections Branch houses the New Mexico Collection featuring books on New Mexico history and culture, and I hoped that would include things about Lawrence. I found a lot of interesting stuff on Ernie Pyle, Dorothy Cline, Lew Wallace and other famous writers with connections to New Mexico. I scanned the books about Lawrence and decided the best two were *D. H. Lawrence in Taos* by Joseph Foster and *D. H. Lawrence in New Mexico* by Arthur J. Bachrach. According to the book jacket, Bachrach owned a bookstore in Taos named Moby Dickens.

And I thought Cocopotamus was a cutesy name.

I read the Foster book and checked out the Bachrach volume because it seemed worthy of more in-depth study. I went outside and stared at the building for a few minutes. Then I retrieved Geronimo and walked home.

A roost of pigeons was scavenging candy wrappers and bits of discarded junk food around the I-25 underpass. With a diet like that, it's no wonder pigeons are fat. They flew up on Geronimo's approach and startled him so thoroughly that he wrapped his lead around me trying to escape them.

There were no customers queued outside my shop, so I passed by and headed up Rio Grande to BookWorks where I bought a volume containing two Lawrence novellas. At the Flying Star Café next door, I ordered their Turkey Jack, a huge sandwich of house-roasted turkey, New Mexico green chile and tomatoes on grilled sourdough. I ate half of it. I was planning on giving the other half to Geronimo who was waiting outside, but I saw him receive half a cupcake and all of a taco from other diners as they left. So I ate the second half. I needed to carb up for the long walk back.

I read the first of the two stories while eating lunch. *St. Mawr* is about a rich woman in the throes of ennui who falls in love with a large unruly mare by that name in whom she sees the unbroken primordial spirit missing in modern man, particularly her husband.

Or something like that. To tell you the truth, reading the thing was giving me a hint of what the throes of ennui must feel like. It was almost as bad as reading Lew Wallace.

Then I got to the part of the book where the daughter leaves her husband in England and goes with the horse to New Mexico where she buys a ranch called *Las Chivas*, which means 'kids'. Not kids in the sense of the young humans I ban from my shop because too many parents let them run wild, but kids in the sense of baby goats.

The woman hires a local to drive her up to see the ranch: "She watched the desert with its tufts of greasewood go lurching past: she saw the fallen apples on the ground in the orchards near the adobe cottages: she looked down into the deep arroyo, and at the stream they forded in the car, and at the mountains blocking up the sky ahead, all with indifference. High on the mountains was snow: lower, blue-grey livid rock: and below the livid rock the aspens were expiring their daffodil-yellow."

I was distracted by the fractured punctuation and eccentric use of adjectives and verbs. I don't think 'expire' can be transitive, but maybe that's why I'm a potter instead of a writer.

But something other than Lawrence's prolixity caught my attention. He was describing New Mexico. And I was pretty certain the ranch he called *Las Chivas* in the story was actually his own ranch above Taos. The Brit who turned English literature on its head was describing my land and using words like '*arroyo*' and '*adobe*' that never passed the lips of Tennyson or Dickens. Somehow, I found the idea fascinating.

I came to the part where they arrive at the cabin on the ranch, and there's a large packrat sitting on the roof staring down at them defiantly as if the ranch is his and they are intruders. The rich woman is offended at the cheek of the rat and, "turning to the Mexican, who was a rag of a man but a pleasant, courteous fellow, she asked him why he didn't shoot the rat. 'Not worth a shell!' said the Mexican, with a faint hopeless smile."

I found myself also with a smile, perhaps faint, but not hopeless. My enthusiasm for reading Lawrence hadn't increased, but my enthusiasm for seeing the ranch where he lived had.

I admit that my primary motivation remained the Duran pot, but now I felt that even if I couldn't find it, the trip might still be worthwhile. That assuaged my conscience somewhat.

10

I had forgotten to buy champagne, so I asked Angie to put a bottle in the cooler so I could take it with me when I left.

She smiled and said, "We always keep one for you, Mr. Schuze," and went to fetch our margaritas.

Susannah said, "The restaurant got an email blast today from the Education Director of the French Wine Society explaining that you shouldn't refer to Gruet as 'champagne'."

"She mentioned me by name?"

"No, silly. And she didn't mention Gruet by name either. She said we shouldn't call American sparkling wines champagne."

"Why not?"

"Because true champagne comes from Champagne, France. Everything else is sparkling wine. It has to do with authenticity. You know, truth in advertising."

"But the Gruet family is from Champagne."

"But the sparkling wine they make here in New Mexico is not."

"It says *méthode champenoise* on the label."

"Yes, but that means it's made *like* champagne, not made *in* Champagne. Like your fakes. You could call them *methode anazasoise*, but they aren't the real deal."

"But nobody can tell the real from the replica. And if they don't ask, I don't tell."

"We're not talking military policy here, Hubie."

"What are we talking about?"

"*Terroir*"

"Dirt?"

"No, a sense of place, the vines giving voice to the soil."

"How many margaritas did you have before I got here?"

"I'm serious. It's like…" She paused and took a sip of her drink. "It's like chiles. Hatch for green, Chimayó for red."

"Well, Gruet does taste like New Mexico."

"They put chiles in it?"

"No, but it has a great nose, as wine people say. It's not as yeasty as some champagnes. It's clean like the desert after a thunderstorm. And it has a hint of cherries. Not the ones in the grocery stores, the ones found along the little river valleys in the Sacramento Mountains around Ruidoso and Cloudcroft."

The wine topic led us to discuss whether tequila has *terroir*. After we agreed the agave gave it *terroir* (or, more appropriately, *tierra*), I told her about the theft from the church.

"You don't suppose someone heard us talking about the theft in Boston and got the idea to—"

"No way," I assured her. "It's just a coincidence."

"How many times do I have to tell you? There are no coincidences, Hubert. That exhibit's been up a while. Why would they do the robbery so shortly after you and I and Martin were talking about art theft?"

"The time they picked didn't have anything to do with our talking about art theft. They didn't know what we were talking about or even that we were talking. They just picked a Thursday, and it just happened to be after our conversation."

She gave me a skeptical look.

11

The next morning was a Saturday, and I left early to drive south to the unnamed dirt road where Emilio and Consuela Sanchez live in a modest adobe, bringing coffee and breakfast burritos. Emilio was waiting outside their residence.

"*Bienvenido, Señor Uberto.*"

"*Buenos dias, Señor Sanchez.*"

"Consuela, she is asleep, but I know she is anxious to see you. I will wake her."

I put a hand on his arm as he turned to go. "She needs her sleep," I said.

He nodded.

We walked around to the back of the house. He had a fire burning in the fifty-five gallon drum he uses as a *parilla*. We sat down close to the warmth and I handed him a coffee. He removed the lid and steam rose around his face as he took a sip.

"It is strong coffee, *amigo*."

I took a sip and nodded my agreement.

When Consuela Saenz came to work for my parents, she was in her late teens. She was not only my nanny (a word I didn't know until many years afterwards), she was also part older sister and part second mother. We left my parents' house in the same year, me to go to college, she to marry. I looked at Emilio and thought she got the better deal. She got a good husband, strong and true. I got kicked out of school for digging pots.

Emilio has worked in the fields for fifty years, his gnarled hands and leathery skin a badge of honest toil. But he was looking drawn and even thinner than his usual sinewy self.

We finished our coffees in silence. I opened the bag and drew out two more along with the burritos.

He smiled. "You could make a *cocinero*. You are always...¿*Como se dice provisionado?*"

"Provisioned," I answered.

"Ah, another word English has taken. It is no wonder your language cover the world. It has...¿*Como se dice adoptó?*"

"Adopted."

He shrugged and smiled. "It has adopted the words of others."

After we had eaten, he turned to me and said, "She grows weaker each day," and he swallowed hard.

"When does Ninfa arrive?"

"Tomorrow. On Monday they make the tests at the hospital to see if her kidney is right." He turned his head away from me and stared out at the pecan trees. "It should be my kidney she receive, *Uberto*. Ninfa is a young woman without even children of her own."

I said nothing. After a minute, he turned back to face me.

"Your kidney is too old, *Viejo*," I said.

He laughed and then dried his eyes with his handkerchief.

We talked a while longer, and I told him to let me know how the tests turned out. I had to cajole the latest doctors' bills from him, and I took them with me when I left. I looked at them when I got home and thought again about the Duran pot.

12

On Sunday afternoon, my nephew Tristan dropped by. He's not actually my nephew. He's the grandson of my mother's sister, my aunt Beatrice, but I call him my nephew and he calls me Uncle Hubert.

I asked him if he'd ever read anything by D. H. Lawrence.

"Sure. We had to read *Sons and Lovers* in soph lit."

"What did you think of it?"

"It was boring. I think the prof said it was a thinly disguised autobiography. I guess he hated his father and loved his mother. Very Freudian."

I told him about my invitation to the Lawrence Ranch, and he seemed excited about it. He told me he could help me with something called a "power point" presentation, and he was so enthusiastic that I agreed to it.

Tristan is always enthusiastic. Also happy and easy-going. He's never lost his layer of baby fat, and his olive skin and dark ringlets of hair seem to entrance young women.

Before he left, I asked him how he was doing and he said he was O.K., so I gave him fifty bucks, and he said he'd come back in a couple of days and teach me about power points. As I watched Tristan strolling away with that loping gait of his, I imagined Ella Fitzgerald singing,

"Just because I always wear a smile- like to dress up in the latest style - cause I'm glad I'm livin'- take troubles all with a smile."

She could have been describing Tristan.

I spent the rest of Sunday and all day Monday in my workshop making replicas. They're easier to sell, and with tourist season approaching, I needed more inventory.

Throwing pots is thirsty work, so I was glad when five o'clock finally rolled around. Susannah asked how things were going with my girlfriend Dolly – she likes romances even more than mysteries.

"She's cooking dinner for me tonight, but to tell you the truth, I'm not too excited about it."

"You don't like her cooking?"

"Her cooking is fine. It's just that she's been moody and argumentative lately, not her usual happy-go-lucky self."

"Maybe she's worried about something. Any changes that would upset her?"

"Her father's health seems to be deteriorating."

"That would more likely make her seek your support rather than bickering with you."

I shrugged. Psychology is not my long suit. "She seems to have gained a bit if weight, but I've never said anything about it."

"Jeez, just like a man. You think the only reason a woman would worry about her weight is because it might affect the man in her life."

"I didn't say that."

"You implied it. Anyway, gaining weight does make a girl moody."

"How would you know? You've never had a weight problem."

She smiled one of her New Mexico sunshine smiles. "When I was in high school, I told my Mom I wanted to look like one of those skinny models. She said it was up to me. So I started dieting. We would sit down to a big dinner and Mom and Dad and my brothers would pile steak, potatoes, beans, and fresh corn on their plates and butter up big chunks of yeasty bread right out of the oven. I'd sit there with cottage cheese and a pear feeling miserable. After about a week, I complained to

Mom that I was hungry all the time, and she said, 'Why do you think those skinny models are never smiling?' That was the end of my diet."

She took a sip of her margarita and changed the subject. "I keep thinking about the theft at the church. You know which one of Quick-To-See Smith's pictures I liked best?"

"Was it *War Shirt 1992*? I liked that one."

"No, it wasn't one of her paintings. It was a photograph she showed in her talk, the one of her as a small girl on the reservation dressed up as Toulouse Lautrec. Remember that one? She said she used grease to paint a beard and mustache on her face. Then she stood on her knees to look short and had someone take her picture." She paused in reflection. "She was so cute in that picture, Hubie. And she's such a nice lady. I hate it that someone stole her work."

Her words hit a little close to home, but I just reminded myself that the people who made the pots I dig up are not losing anything.

13

I met Dolly Madison Aguirre when I was going door to door in *Casitas del Bosque* looking for a house I had visited while blindfolded. I'll spare you the details. Turns out her father had been my history teacher at Albuquerque High School. One thing led to another, as it usually does, and we ended up dating.

I showed up at Dolly's now-familiar front door at ten past seven and rang the bell. Judging from how quickly she opened the door, she must have been standing behind it.

It was not because she was anxious to see me.

"You're late," she said.

"Sorry," I said and leaned in to kiss her.

"If you don't think enough of me to show up on time, just don't bother," she said and closed the door in my face.

She had been moody for the past several weeks, but nothing like this. I stood there on the porch debating whether to ring the bell again. I decided against it and drove home. My phone was ringing when I opened the door.

"I'm sorry, Hubie," said Dolly when I answered. "I overreacted. Will you come back? I have a nice meal all ready."

I told her I would and drove back. She gave me a passionate kiss at the door, but once we sat down for the meal, she berated me for not having a cell phone.

"The food is cold. I could have called you as you were driving, but I had to wait until you got all the way home. Why don't you have a cell phone like everyone else?"

I told her I would get one if she wanted me to, hoping that she wouldn't because I really hate the idea of being at the beck and call of everyone on the planet at any time of the night or day.

My response seemed to satisfy her, and the rest of the meal was spent in small talk. Then she suggested that I get ready for bed while she did the dishes. She knows I don't like sleeping over at her house because her father is in the next room. Call me old-fashioned, but it bothers me. But given her moodiness, I didn't want to refuse the invitation.

I was in bed when she returned from the kitchen. After going through her usual evening routine, she slipped in next to me wearing nothing but the scent of gardenias. We kissed passionately for quite some time, but then something happened.

Or, more accurately, something didn't happen. I knew it was because her father was next door, but she had a different explanation.

She started sobbing. "You don't want to make love because I'm fat."

I held her awkwardly until she calmed down. "You are not fat. I love having sex with you. Surely you know that after all these months. I'm just inhibited by being one room away from your father."

She started kissing me again, but I realized another failure would only reinforce her view that I no longer found her attractive.

"Come back to my place," I suggested.

She rolled on her side and said, "Go home."

14

I slept fitfully.

Emilio showed up Tuesday morning with the good news that his daughter's kidney was a match and could be transplanted into her mother. At least I thought it was good news, but then I wasn't facing the prospect of both my wife and my daughter undergoing major surgery.

Tristan, Susannah and I had all been rejected as donors, not surprising given that we are from different gene pools, but each of us had insisted on being tested. I figured I have two kidneys so I wouldn't miss one of them. It's not like I had given them pet names or anything.

It was obvious Emilio was still digesting the news and fretting, so I decided to change the subject. I asked him if he had ever heard of D. H. Lawrence.

His eyes lit up. "*Claro*," he said, "everyone in my secondary school was made to read *La serpiente con plumas*."

What an odd quirk of translation, I thought to myself. I had read in *D. H. Lawrence in Taos* that Lawrence titled *The Plumed Serpent* after *Quetzalcoatl*, the mythical beast of the Aztecs. In Spanish, the book should therefore be called simply *Quetzalcoatl*. But the publisher evidently chose to translate the English back into Spanish literally.

The title was all I knew of the book, so I asked Emilio what it was about.

"I have forgotten most of what I learn in school, but I remember that book because I thought it was about the *agraristas* of Michoacán. My grandfather was one of them."

"Who were the *agraristas*?"

"Mr. Lawrence did not call them by that name. Some said they were communists. Others said they were *fascistas*. I do not know about these things. I know only that they wished to stop the changes the *conquistadores* brought to Mexico. They fight against the Church, and they want people to live on the land like before the Spanish come."

"Did you like the book?"

"I am a *camposino*, Uberto. I do not understand such books."

"I would value your opinion," I said.

He nodded and sat for a moment in thought. "I did not like the book because the *narradora* was a woman from Ireland, and she see the Mexican people as uncivilized. I think she is unhappy with civilization, so when she say the Mexicans are uncivilized, she say it as something good. But I don't think it is good. I was young and proud to be a Mexican."

"And now?"

His leathery face formed into a smile. "Now I am old and proud to be a Mexican. We are Indians and Spaniards both, and we should be proud of both parts."

Emilio departed after presenting me with a large sack of *carne adobado*. I rolled some of it into corn tortillas and enjoyed tacos for lunch with a couple of cold Cabaña beers from El Salvador. Globalization.

15

Which accounts for the fact that I was asleep when Tristan arrived later that afternoon.

Turns out that what I had been calling power point is actually PowerPoint™. In addition to photographing some of my pots for the trademarked whiz bang software, Tristan also brought two books. He handed me a beat-up, yellowing Penguin paperback called *D. H. Lawrence – Selected Letters* and told me to read the letter on page 146. It was addressed to Catherine Carswell and dated 18 May, 1924.

Lawrence wrote, "Did I tell you Mabel Lujan gave Frieda that little ranch – about 160 acres – up here in the skirts of the mountains? We have been up there the last fortnight working like the devil, with 3 Indians and a Mexican carpenter, building up the 3-room log cabin, which was falling down. We've done all the building, save the chimney – and we've made the adobe bricks for that. I hope in the coming week to finish everything, shingling the roofs of the other cabins too. There are two log cabins, a 3-roomer for us, a 2-roomer Mabel can have when she comes, a little one-roomer for Brett – and a nice log hay-house and corral. We have four horses in the clearing. It is very wild, with the pine-trees coming down the mountain – and the altitude, 8,600 ft., takes a bit of getting used to. But it is also very fine."

Dorothy Brett was a British painter associated with the Bloomsbury group. She came to Taos at Lawrence's invitation and remained there for the rest of her life.

I looked up at Tristan inquisitively.

He shrugged. "I'm dating an English major."

"She gave you this?"

"Loaned it to me. I told her you were going to the Lawrence Ranch, and she said you might like to know what D. H. himself said about it. She attended the annual writer's conference they have up there every summer and is sort of hooked on Lawrence. She's thinking of writing her MA on him, but her advisor is against it. He says too much has already been done on Lawrence, and she'd be better off to pick someone less well-known where there's at least some chance of doing something fresh."

"She have anyone in mind?"

"Witter Bynner."

"She should qualify as lesser known. I've never heard of her."

"It's a him, and I'd never heard of him either until Emily told me about him. She picked him because he had a connection with Lawrence, and she didn't want to get completely away from that. She's fascinated by the whole Taos Circle thing."

"I think I'm developing the same fascination. What was Bynner's connection with Lawrence?"

"Well, they may have been lovers."

"What! Lawrence was married."

"Come on, Uncle Hubert. Even you must have heard of bisexuals. Anyway, Bynner was definitely gay. He taught poetry at the University of California around the time of the First World War and often held his classes in hotel rooms. The University took a dim view of that and dismissed him. He ended up in Santa Fe sharing a house with Spud Johnson."

"There's a name," I said. "I read about him in *D. H. Lawrence in Taos*. He was Mabel Dodge's secretary."

"Right. He introduced Bynner to Dodge, who eventually accused Bynner of single-handedly introducing homosexuality into New

Mexico. Emily said she isn't sure if Dodge meant that remark as an insult or a compliment. Anyway, it was through her that Bynner met Frieda and D. H., and he traveled with them to Mexico where it's rumored he and Lawrence had an affair. Emily says that Bynner and Spud Johnson are two of the characters in the novel Lawrence set in Mexico, *The Plumed Serpent*."

That sound you just heard was my jaw hitting the *piñon* floor. "Unbelievable. Just this morning Emilio told me he had to read the *Plumed Serpent* in secondary school in Mexico."

"Emily says it's Lawrence's greatest work."

"Have you read it?"

"Nah, I don't read much. But I'm getting a great introduction to lit from Emily. It's a lot more fun hearing her talk about Lawrence than it would be to read him."

"Easier too."

"Definitely. Two more things about Bynner."

"What?"

"First, the house he lived in in Santa Fe is still there, and it's now a gay bed and breakfast."

"What does that mean? Straight people can't stay there?"

He shrugged. "I don't think the object is to exclude straights. It's more a matter of creating a gay-friendly environment."

"Oh. And the second thing?"

He handed me the second book, another collection of Lawrence's letters. The guy was a letter-writing machine. The letter Tristan directed me to was on page 48 and was addressed to Bynner and dated 19 July, 1924.

It read, "Dear Bynner, we are at the height of the New Mexico summer. We bake during the day and freeze at night. Poor D. H., perfectly miserable. I would trade for steamy Mexico and the dirty Zocalo peddlers. We rode yesterday to Mabel and Tony but did not stay. She was ranting and at least it is cooler up here. The ranch is primitive but stirs me. The only refinement is a new pot brought by a Mexican named Duran. It was full of a beef stew too hot to eat, but the pot is beautiful. It is what they call an 'olla' and is signed. Mabel was furious with jealousy when she heard the news."

Tristan said, "I thought the reference to a pot would interest you even though it was Mexican instead of Indian."

"It isn't Mexican. Lawrence is wrong. Duran was a potter from the Taos Pueblo."

I told Tristan I needed a crash course on Lawrence in New Mexico, especially anything having to do with the cabin. He arranged for me to meet with Emily the next day, and we spent four hours going over the materials she had collected for her thesis.

After the four hours passed, I had learned three things. First, writing a thesis must be excruciatingly dull work. Second, judging from all the questions she asked, Emily was more interested in Tristan than she was in Lawrence. Finally, the pot had been in the cabin on Lawrence's last day there. Among the many copies of photos Emily showed me was one on which someone, probably Frieda, had scribbled, "D. H. departing again" and the date of his last trip from New Mexico. A venture from which he would never return.

Unless you count his ashes. After Lawrence died, Frieda had a memorial for him built at the Ranch. Then she sent Angelo Ravagli, her Italian lover and later third husband, to Europe to have Lawrence' body exhumed and cremated. Ravagli was supposed to bring the ashes back to New Mexico, but rumor has it that he dumped them in the Atlantic.

But he did bring some ashes back, and Frieda planned to place them in the memorial. Mabel Dodge Luhan and The Brett (as she was called) wanted to scatter the ashes over the ranch. Perhaps because she always had to compete against those two for Lawrence's attention, Frieda dumped the ashes into a wheelbarrow containing wet cement and said, "Now let's see them steal this!" The cement was used to make the memorial's altar.

I stared at the photo. Lawrence looks impatient. There is a knapsack in his left hand and a walking stick in his right. And on a table behind him the pot – or one very similar to it – sits next to an oil lamp.

Lawrence kept the pot for two years. But that was eighty years ago. Perhaps Frieda threw it out, gave it away or accidentally broke it. But there was also a chance it was still there.

16

I walked over to *Dos Hermanas* at five eager to tell Susannah about the Taos pot.

But while I was trying to signal our favorite dark and sultry waitress, Susannah started telling me she had decided to give up computer dating and let love come to her rather than she to it.

"So there's a big event at the Millicent Rogers Museum and all the art history faculty and students are invited. I've decided to go. I've got to get out and mix, Hubie. Are you definitely going to the event at the Lawrence Ranch?"

"I am."

"Then maybe you can give me a ride to Taos? The reception is this Friday night. Isn't that when your event starts?"

"Actually, its starts at noon with a lecture on Lawrence, but I'm skipping that part and showing up for the cocktail party Friday night. My dog and pony show is the next morning at 10:00, but I won't be coming back until Sunday afternoon. Will you be in Taos that long?"

"Just overnight. You remember Ellie?"

"The ditzy blond with all the turquoise jewelry?"

"She's not ditzy, Hubie. You just say that because she's blond."

I shrugged.

"She's from Taos and she's already up there. I'll stay with her and then come back on Saturday, so I only need you to take me up there."

"I'll enjoy the company. You know how I hate to travel."

"You're sure it's no trouble?"

"None at all. The ranch is about thirty miles north of Taos, so I have to pass right by the Rogers Museum on the way."

I told her what Lawrence had written in his letter to Bynner. Then I told her who Bynner was and that he had lived in Santa Fe with Spud Johnson who was Mabel Dodge's secretary. She told me Millicent Rogers and Mabel Dodge had a stormy relationship during their years in Taos, two fabulously wealthy heiresses from back east, each wanting to be the Queen Bee. Susannah told me that Rogers described her relationship with Dodge as a "fight with a knife in each hand." Then she asked me what was so special about the pot Lawrence had described.

"Traditional Taos pots were not fancy, so no one collected them. Finding one made prior to 1970 is rare. Finding an old one that is signed is unheard of."

"Why is it shiny?"

"Taos potters used clay with mica in it. That's why the pot glinted in the sunlight."

"Do you think the pot is still there at the ranch?"

"I have no idea. The letter to Bynner was written eighty years ago."

"But it could still be there?"

"Anything is possible."

"And you'd like to find it."

"I would."

She gave me that enigmatic smile. "How much would that pot be worth?"

I had been thinking about that ever since I read the letter, but I didn't have an answer. "There are no actual sales to base an estimate on because there aren't any for sale, so I don't really know."

"But you could make an educated guess?"

"Like everything else, the rarer a pot, the higher the price. I would have to find out how well Duran was known as a potter, how much work he did, things like that. But any eighty-year-old Taos pot signed by the potter would have to be worth twenty-five thousand. Maybe more."

"You've had other pots worth that."

"True. But what I just said was 'any eighty-year-old Taos pot signed by the potter would have to be worth twenty-five thousand'. But this is not just *any* pot. This is a pot associated with one of the most famous writers of all time."

"Or infamous."

"Right. A five-carat diamond is worth a lot. But a five-carat diamond worn by Mae West is worth even more."

"So how much would the Lawrence connection add to the price?"

"I'm over my head here, Suze. But it could be double."

"Fifty thousand!"

"Of course I couldn't sell the pot. I'd have to give it to Cyril Duran. But the three Dulcineas he promised in return would be worth even more."

"Why are hers more valuable than his? Are they more authentic in some way?"

"No. In fact, they're less authentic because they were made on a wheel rather than by the traditional method of moving your hand instead of the pot."

"I don't get it. Why would an inauthentic pot be worth more?"

I thought about that for a minute. "It shouldn't be. You know I deal only with traditional designs, so authenticity is important to me."

"Even in your fakes?" she chided.

"Especially in my fakes. If they don't look totally authentic, no one will buy them."

She laughed, and I said, "You're the art historian. I should be asking you about authenticity and the value of art."

"Well, there is an important issue about how a dominant culture or class determines what art should be produced."

"The Golden Rule," I quipped.

"Right, he who has the gold makes the rules. Unfortunately, it's true. You know about the *Pachamama*?"

"Only that she's a South American mother earth and fertility goddess."

"Right. When the Spaniards converted the natives to Christianity, the Indians saw the Virgin Mary as the white man's *Pachamama*. The priests didn't object because it made the conversions easier if you didn't force the Indians to give up all their former images."

"O.K., but what does that have to do with authenticity?"

"Pre-Columbian renderings of the *Pachamama* show a female-like character in the shape of a mountain. But after the Spanish came, the Indians painted her with a halo and western clothes. And those are the ones that sell today."

"Same type of thing here," I noted. "Some of the designs on the Indian rugs they sell right here in Old Town are of European origin and were introduced to the weavers by the priests."

I noticed we were out of chips and salsa, so I waved for Angie. The replenishments must have spurred Susannah to another train of thought because when they arrived, she said, "It's not just in art. The first server job I had was at the Chew Din Café. I admitted to the owner when I applied for the job that I didn't know anything about Chinese food. He said, 'That's O.K. We don't serve Chinese food,' and then he cackled. He explained that their recipes were designed to please the locals and didn't taste anything like the food in China."

I loaded a chip with salsa, lofted my margarita and made a toast to authenticity.

17

The New Mexico spring was doing its yo-yo routine, and the day had been surprisingly warm. Dolly showed up at seven that evening in a colorful broomstick skirt and a white loose-fitting blouse. When we hugged, I could tell there was no other clothing under the blouse. Her hello kiss portended a pleasant evening.

We went to the kitchen, and I offered her a chilled flute of Gruet.

She took a sip and said, "Nice and cold."

I smiled.

Then she said, "But your house is like an oven."

"It must be from the cooking. But I turned on the air conditioner, so it should cool down."

She held a hand up towards the vent. "Why isn't the air colder?" she asked in an assertive tone.

I sensed another argument developing and decided to head it off by being agreeable. "I guess because my air-conditioner is an old-fashioned evaporative cooler."

"Why don't you get refrigerated cooling?" she challenged.

Agreeable wasn't working. So I tried humor. "I'm trying to maintain a small carbon footprint."

"What the hell does that mean?"

I shrugged and smiled.

"I'm going outside," she said.

"It's warm out there, too."

"I know that. I just came in from out there, remember?" Then she stomped out to the patio.

Dolly likes salads, so I prepared a large one with frisée, cucumbers, tomatoes, diced poblano peppers, fresh cilantro, sugared pecans and dried cranberries. Not my usual New Mexican cuisine, but light with a touch of the Southwest. The dressing was avocado oil and lemon juice. I was putting the salad on the table when she returned.

"Well, it feels a little cooler in here."

Of course it does, I was tempted to say. You just spent five minutes with the desert sun blasting you from the west. It's the feeling-cooler version of the feeling-better method of hitting yourself with a hammer because it feels so good when it stops hurting.

The salad course went well.

When I brought the hot tray of chicken enchiladas to the table, Dolly took off her blouse. I, too, thought they smelled terrific, but I didn't realize the aroma was *that* good.

She saw my jaw drop and explained she was hot again. "Do you mind if I sit here like this?" she asked in a tone halfway between defiant and flirtatious.

Frankly, I thought it was a bit odd. Dolly and I had been sleeping together for almost a year, so there was no reason for either of us to feel uncomfortable because her blouse was off. But I did feel uncomfortable.

I know "topless" women draw men like trailer houses attract tornadoes. How else do you explain "topless" barber shops, "topless" shoeshine stands, "topless" sports bars, etc? I think the entire concept is bizarre. I like seeing a woman "topless" or – even better – completely nude. But why would I want a woman with bare breasts to cut my hair or shine my shoes? Wouldn't she be embarrassed? I know I would be.

And that was the way I was feeling at that moment even though it was Dolly and not some total stranger.

After dinner we went to bed where we were both properly attired in nothing. She was sweating like a Swede in a sauna, and caressing her felt like being a contestant in one of those greased pig contests. I know that sounds terrible, but that's what came to mind.

Evidently no other thoughts came to mind, especially no romantic ones, because the same thing that happened the last time I was at her house happened again at my house.

Or didn't happen.

She started crying. "You don't find me sexy anymore."

"Don't be ridiculous. I know you're hot and uncomfortable, and that distracts me. I'm worried about you."

She sobbed for another thirty seconds, and then looked at me with a little-girl smile and asked, "Do you want me to go home?"

"Of course not."

"You really don't think I'm too fat?"

"You're just the same as when we first met. I liked you then. I like you even more now."

18

Yesterday's heat had disappeared on Friday morning. A chill wind was blowing from the north.

Tristan came by at noon to make sure everything was set up for my PowerPoint. After he checked the computer and the projector, he gave me a spare bulb and showed me how to change it in case the one in there burned out. Changing the bulb looked easy, but technology has a way of turning on me without warning, so even the mention of a burned out bulb made me uneasy. The most complicated piece of machinery I normally operate is my kiln which has only an on/off switch and a dial to set the temperature.

I loaded the equipment and my bag, pillow, sheets, and a box full of peanuts. The Styrofoam sort. Nestled inside the peanuts and protected by them was a twelve-hundred-year-old Anasazi pot I found without digging in the ground. It had been partially buried under a lot of bat guano in what I am pretty sure was a grain storage bin in an ancient cliff-dwelling that no one knows about other than me and the original inhabitants who no longer had need of the pot since they've been dead for over a thousand years.

Tristan told me he would be in his apartment in the morning before my presentation, and I could call him if I needed any help. I told him the brochure the University sent me about the Ranch said phone service tended to be intermittent, so he handed me a cell phone.

"You don't expect me to use this, do you?"

He chuckled. "I'll program in my land line number. Even you can use it then."

All I had to do was push one button. I accepted the contraption with misgivings. It startled me by ringing just after he left, but I quickly realized it was my own phone. I picked up the receiver, and Dolly said she was outside and just wanted to wish me luck in Taos. I invited her in, but she said she was in a hurry, so I went out to the curb where she was parked with the engine running and the air-conditioning on despite the fact that the air had again plummeted into the frosty range.

My first thought on seeing her wedged behind the wheel was that the real reason she didn't come in was it would take the jaws-of-life to get her out of the car. It looked like she had gained another stone since I saw her.

"I'm going to Bernalillo," she said. "You want to follow along as you head north?"

"Thanks for the offer, but I have to swing by and pick up Susannah."

"You didn't tell me Susannah was going," she said in a tone that made me uneasy.

"It was a last minute decision."

"I hope you and your girlfriend have a great time. Don't bother to call me when you get back."

I was stunned. "Susannah and I are just friends. *You* are my girlfriend."

"Right," she said sarcastically. "You won't even make love to me."

"But I told you why—"

"Forget it. The real reason why I don't want to see you anymore is you stole my dog." Then she spattered me with gravel as she spun the wheels on her departure.

On the way to pick up Susannah, I tried to figure out whether I should tell her about Dolly's dramatic visit.

When she placed her things in the back of the Bronco next to mine, she laughed and said, "A pillow and sheets?"

"Well," I replied, "who knows what sort of bedding they have up there? I can't sleep if my pillow isn't just right."

"Are you bringing your blankie, too?"

I was, as a matter of fact.

We kept up the banter all the way to the Cochiti Pueblo with its casino sitting incongruously in the desert like a garish string of costume jewelry around the neck of the Virgin Mary. As we started up the escarpment towards Santa Fe, the air turned even colder, and Susannah turned the heater up to full blast.

Just south of Santa Fe, we began to see snowflakes. When we got north of town, the few flakes turned into flurries, and by the time we reached Taos, the snow was falling so heavily that I had to slow down to about thirty miles an hour because of limited visibility. We crept through Taos which looked almost deserted and drove north to the Millicent Rogers Museum which looked totally deserted.

And was, the only sign of recent human presence being a sign on the door saying the event scheduled for that evening had been cancelled because of the inclement weather. I offered to take Susannah back to Ellie's house, but she said she didn't know where Ellie lived, so we went to the La Fonda Hotel on the Plaza and borrowed their phone book to look up Ellie's address.

A stooped old clerk wearing a coat made from a Navaho blanket slapped the book on the counter. Just as she opened it, Susannah remembered that Ellie lived with her mother who had remarried, and she didn't know her stepfather's last name. Susannah, that is. I assume Ellie knew it, although given how ditzy she is, I wouldn't have bet on it.

Susannah also didn't have Ellie's phone number. They had agreed to meet at the Museum, so Susannah didn't think to bring the number with her. She thought the number had 459 in it and maybe started with a 2, and she punched in several numbers at a payphone next to the counter, but that turned out to be as useful as you would expect.

"So now what?" I asked.

"I guess I'll just have to get a room here until Sunday, and you can pick me up on your way back to Albuquerque."

The room clerk retrieved his phone book and said, "We don't have any rooms."

"There are other places," said Susannah.

"All full," said the clerk. "We've had a string of travelers in here all day because of the storm. I called all the other places for them after we filled up. There ain't a room left anywhere."

"It doesn't matter," I said. "I couldn't let you waste time and money staying here all weekend. I'll just drive you back to Albuquerque."

"No you won't," said the clerk with what sounded to me like a good deal of impertinence.

"Why not?"

"Because the Highway Patrol closed the road south of town fifteen minutes ago. I heard it on the radio."

The clerk was full of information I didn't want to hear, and even though I was sure he was right, I didn't want to continue our discussion in his presence. So I took Susannah by the arm and led her over to a couch at the opposite end of the lobby where we sat down to decide what to do.

Which, after a good deal of discussion, was to go on to the Ranch. It was the only place where I knew I would have a room, and I figured they might have an extra one for Susannah as well. If not, she could stay in my room, and I'd sleep on the floor. The sheets and pillow I brought would come in handy.

The only problem would be getting there. If they had closed the road going south back towards Santa Fe and Albuquerque, they would certainly have closed the one going north where the storm was even worse. And they had. A patrol car with flashing lights was parked just north of the Rogers Museum. I made a right before I got that far, drove towards the big mountain, then turned left on a small dirt road. I got out and locked the front hubs then shifted into four wheel drive and plowed slowly down the road for about five miles, which took fifteen minutes because I could only go twenty miles an hour. Then I turned left and was soon back on the main road where the going was a little easier, but it still took us two hours to reach the turnoff to the Ranch. Then the going really got fun.

Presumably, there was a road, but it had long since disappeared under the snow. We had a general idea of where it was – somewhere between the tops of the scrub pines we could see to the right and the left. What else lay between those trees we could only guess. Ditches? Culverts? Boulders?

I spend a lot of time in remote places searching for pots, and I'm a cautious sort of fellow, so I keep warm clothes, extra batteries, water, a candle, matches, and other essential supplies in the back of the Bronco. I put on most of the clothing, including hightop insulated boots and heavy gloves. I took out a long thin piece of rebar I use for probing in the dirt and used it to poke into the snow to locate the edge of the road. Then I walked the three miles to the Conference Center with Susannah driving slowly behind me. When we were about five hundred yards from the Conference Center, I saw ruts in the deep snow headed off at an angle to the right and was confused. I poked around with the rebar and determined that we should continue straight ahead, and we did so, with me silently cursing the delay when we were almost there. I trudged on like Nanook of the North and finally arrived seven hours after leaving Albuquerque at a place you can normally drive to in three hours.

I was tired, cold, hungry, and thirsty.

19

The warm yellow glow from the windows in the Conference Center and the smoke from its chimney conveyed a warm and well-deserved welcome.

The two men who met us at the door conveyed anything but.

The first was Chauncey Benthrop, a name he pronounced as if we should know it. He added that he was a Full Professor of Literature at the University of New Mexico, placing heavy emphasis on the word "full."

Benthrop was a couple of inches taller than me but thinner, with a drawn face and a long pinched nose with nostrils that looked like coin slots. His brown hair was in a ponytail and his pointed chin was only slightly obscured by a wispy Fu Man Chu. He had long yellow teeth that showed when he said, "Who might you be?"

He was wearing brown corduroy slacks and a darker brown cable sweater. His hand held a glass of brown liquid, Scotch if the color was any indication. I didn't like his clothes, his beard, his looks, or his officious manner. I don't like Scotch either, but I didn't hold that against him. What I disliked most of all was being kept out in the snow.

"I might be Dashiell Hammett," I said, forcing my way past him. Susannah slid in behind me.

The second man was Charles Winant, a rotund man with a prominent belly and a head like a gourd with two cold blue eyes under black shiny hair combed straight back. He wore dark slacks and a heavy red turtleneck sweater. I asked him if he was also on the program like Full Professor Benthrop, and he said he was not.

"Oh," I said, "then you must be a donor to the University."

"Certainly not!" he replied emphatically. "The University is a den of iniquity. They promote gambling with so-called 'casino nights' in their dorms. Students should be taught that God rewards hard work, not games of chance. Benthrop here works there but he sees the truth – our civilization is crumbling. I tell you, Hammett, Armageddon is near."

"My name isn't Hammett. It's Hubert Schuze. I'm doing a presentation tomorrow on Indian pottery."

"I distinctly heard you tell Benthrop your name is Hammett."

"I didn't say my name is Hammett. He asked who I *might* be, and I said I might be Hammett."

"Only a philistine could misunderstand me," Benthrop huffed.

"Do you specialize in the literature of the ancient Middle East?" I asked. When he didn't get it, I felt smug. I know it was sophomoric, but Benthrop deserved it. I said nothing more. I was supposed to entertain these dignitaries, not argue with them. I decided to suffer these two fools, though I can't say I did so gladly.

Winant was holding what looked to be a printed program, and he looked up from it to say, "There is no mention here of your wife accompanying you."

"This is Susannah Inchaustigui," I said. "She is not my wife."

"Then who is she?" he demanded. "I certainly hope you haven't introduced a harlot into our midst."

Susannah's big eyes narrowed as she opened her mouth, but I shot her a glance, and she said nothing. I was trying to frame a suitable response when we were rescued by a tall blonde lady with a pixie haircut and a wide mouth.

"Pay no attention to these two old grouches," she said and gave Winant a friendly poke in the tummy. He drew back as if her finger were a rapier.

We had entered a foyer with a bench and a coat rack. Through an arched opening we could see people milling about in the large main room with vinyl floor tiles and high ceilings. The appeal of high ceilings was offset by the fact they were finished with acoustic tile.

On the front wall was a large fireplace made of smooth round rocks, and in it burned a pile of split *piñon* logs. The walls were the earth brown of traditional New Mexico stucco but they were obviously made of gypsum board. I suppose it's difficult to give a large public space a sense of style, but this one seemed even more institutional than most modern attempts to capture the pueblo style. Still, it was warm and bright, and we were happy to be there.

"I'm Betty Shanile," our rescuer said, "and you two need food and drink."

She led us to a table laden with both. There were bottles of all the most popular beverages except champagne, alas. There were glasses and a bucket of ice. Susannah selected white wine. I filled a squat tumbler with ice and poured myself a generous portion of Old Granddad, just the fellow I needed to warm my insides.

I judged Betty to be in her mid-fifties. I first believed her cheeks to be naturally rosy and her lips naturally red, but nobody is born with blue skin above their eyes, so I concluded it was expertly applied make-up. She had a natural smile, casual clothes that looked expensive, and a wedding ring set with a diamond the size of a grape. She leaned over to whisper to me and her perfume was intoxicating.

"Who is the young lady?"

"Her name is Susannah Inchaustigui. She was supposed to attend an event at the Millicent Rogers Museum, but it was cancelled because of the snow. She had nowhere to stay, so I brought her here."

"Aren't you the gentleman. And do you work at the University like Full Professor Chauncey Benthrop?"

When she said that, I knew I was going to like her. We both laughed at the way she included his title. I told her I didn't work at the University.

"Where do you work, Hubie? You don't mind if I call you Hubie, do you?"

I told her I didn't mind, although I did just a little because I'm not all that good at getting to know people, and I guess maybe I like the reassurance of a little formality with people I've known for all of five minutes. I told her I wasn't employed anywhere, and she asked me what I did to make a living. I told her that now and then I sell a pot, which is a pretty accurate description of my business.

"Where do you get the pots?"

Given that some of my inventory is acquired illegally, I'm always cautious about how I answer that question when it is posed by someone I don't know well, so I gave an evasive response. "Oh," I said, "some of them I've had for years. In fact, I sometimes hate to sell them. I guess I'm attached to them, but—"

She gave me a little squeeze and said, "Isn't that touching?"

Then she picked up two empty wine bottles and clanked them together, and when everyone turned at the sound, she said, "Everyone, this is Hubert Schuze, but he likes to be called Hubie."

I cringed.

She continued. "He's going through a bit of a rough patch economically...well, he's actually not working at the moment, and he has to sell pots that have been in his family for years just to make ends meet, but he's the perfect gentleman. This young lady is Susannah, and he met her tonight at the Rogers Museum where she was stranded, so he brought her here."

Susannah was looking at me as if I had lost my mind. I started to say something to the dozen or so people in the room, but they all started lining up to introduce themselves. Susannah chides me about reading books that have neither interesting fictional stories nor practical information. My usual two defenses are that learning is its own reward and that you can't know in advance what information might turn out to be useful. Sandwiched between books by and about Lawrence, I had been reading *Moonwalking with Einstein: The Art and Science of Remembering Everything* by Joshua Foer. It contained the fascinating story of Simonides of Ceos, a 5th century B.C. poet who was to be the speaker at a banquet in Thessalia. Just before the event was to begin, he was summoned outside by a messenger. While he was receiving the message, the building collapsed, and everyone inside was killed. Because they were crushed under heavy marble, there was no way to identify the corpses. Family members couldn't figure out who they should bury. Then Simonides realized he knew exactly where everyone was seated. Foer called this event 'The Beginning of Memory'.

Simonides' method is known today as the memory palace technique, a mnemonic device for remembering sequences based on spatial relationships. Simonides remembered who was seated to his left, who was seated at the table across from him, the location of the tall attractive woman, who was on her right, etc. Of course it's one thing to remember spatial relationships you have actually seen but quite another to remember ones that you invent. Yet it is the invented ones that are the key to the memory palace technique. You can memorize a sequence of unrelated things – a list of names, for example – by creating a 'mental walk', placing the items from the list on a familiar path.

Suppose I had to memorize the menu at *La Placita* and the items were cheese enchiladas, beef enchiladas, chicken enchiladas, tacos and beans. I imagine myself walking through my house after I wake up. The first place I go is the bathroom. I imagine a big triangular slab of cheese on the floor serving as a doorstop. Then I move to the toilet but there is a big cow sitting on it. I turn to the sink to brush my teeth and there is a chicken nesting in the lavatory. I go to the kitchen to make coffee and the coffee filter is bent into the shape of a taco. Of course the coffee beans turn out to be pintos.

Memorizing cheese enchiladas, beef enchiladas, chicken enchiladas, tacos and beans is not that difficult. But I would probably forget the order within a few hours. But the memory walk I just described could be recalled days or even months later. I know this because it's the sequence I used to test the technique, and now I can't forget it even though I want to. Every time I go to the bathroom, I see that damn cow on my toilet.

I decided to use the technique to memorize the names of the people at the Ranch.

The first person in the impromptu receiving line was a tall dark man with large limpid eyes and a full head of hair combed into a pompadour.

"Srinivasa Patel," he said with a broad smile and a thick accent as he shook my hand vigorously.

"Pleased to meet you," I said. "About my pot selling—"

"The less said the better, right? At least you have something to sell. I believe you have a saying in America, 'He doesn't have a pot to...' well, I shouldn't say the rest."

"What do you do, Mr. Patel?"

"Please call me Srini. I work for the University of New Mexico."

"In fund-raising?"

He laughed. "Oh, no. I know nothing of that."

"Are you on the faculty?"

"Technically, yes. But I'm currently on leave. I actually teach—"

I didn't find out what he taught because a tall man with silver hair and a golden tan pried my hand away from Srini and introduced himself as Robert Saunders.

"The pots I sell—" I started.

"Are your own," he finished for me, although that was not what I was going to say. "I was a judge for many years before I retired. I can assure you that selling pot is illegal." He slapped me on the back. "But selling pots isn't."

While he was laughing at his little joke, I started to question his comment on the legality of selling pots. "Well, there is a law called the Archaeological Resources Protection Act."

He shook his head. "Totally unenforceable unless they catch you in the act. If possession of an artifact were a crime, half the people in New Mexico would be in prison. I finally had to tell prosecutors not to clutter my docket with those cases because I was going to summarily dismiss all of them."

I smiled at him. "Too bad you retired."

The next person in the impromptu receiving line was Fred Rich, a big guy in a golf shirt with hairy arms and meaty hands. He had the kind of facial hair you have to shave twice a day. I could tell he had just finished his second because his cheap aftershave smelled like it had just been splashed on, and he had two little pieces of toilet paper stuck to places where he had nicked himself. He told me he was in the "fast food game" and was always looking for talent. I told him I wasn't really looking for a job. Especially flipping burgers, I thought to myself, but he said I'd have to work sooner or later.

"When you run out of pots, what will you do? Start selling off the furniture?"

No answer came to mind, so that was the one I gave. He handed me his card and moved away.

I gave up. I decided I would explain the whole thing at the start of my presentation in the morning when they were a captive audience. So I just stood there and smiled when Carla Glain introduced herself and said I was just getting a small taste of what women had faced for centuries, exclusion from the workplace and having to rely on handicrafts to eke out a living. I smiled at her and said I agreed completely.

Once I stopped stressing over the confusion caused by Betty's announcement, I began to relax. Of course the Old Granddad also helped. I met Teodoro Vasquez, a lobbyist.

"I can help you network," he said. "I know everyone in New Mexico who is anyone."

I smiled and thanked him, thinking that since he didn't know me, that made me no one, which was fine with me.

Vasquez was followed by Howard Glover, a giant of a man with onyx skin, a shaved head, and muscles in places where I don't even have places.

"I own car dealerships throughout the state. If you can sell pots, selling cars would be a snap. It's all on commission, of course, but our top salespersons make big bucks."

His handshake was so strong that I almost offered to buy a car if he would let go. When he finally did, I checked my hand for broken fingers and told him I'd keep him in mind.

Glover was followed by Agatha Cruz who, in contrast to Betty Shanile, had terrible powdery-looking make-up that failed to conceal the wrinkles on her face. She also smelled worse. Betty wore an expensive perfume that was beguiling without being overpowering. Agatha smelled of antiseptic. She said she didn't feel well and was tired. She retired to her room shortly after we met.

Charles Winant was next and he asked me again about Susannah. I explained again that we were just friends. He nodded and asked, "Have you found Jesus, Hammett?"

"I didn't even know he was missing," I replied. I didn't want to be sacrilegious, but I have a low tolerance for zealots.

He gave me a hard stare and turned away.

The last person in line was Carl Wron, an elderly rancher with leathery skin and thinning hair. Which is certainly better than leathery hair and thinning skin. He did not offer me a job herding cattle or tending sheep. He wore a western shirt with a string tie and a belt with a buckle the size of a saucer.

"Are you a donor, Mr. Wron?"

"Oh, I give a little something now and again."

I was guessing it was more than a little something. A check for a hundred bucks doesn't get you invited to a weekend retreat.

"Is your ranch around here?"

"No, it's on the east side of the mountains. It's a good thing I don't have to get home for anything. I don't reckon I could make it across the passes in this storm."

I had now met everyone in the room except a plump young woman standing behind the drinks table and a fellow in an ill-fitting red blazer. To be precise, I should call it a cherry-colored blazer. Cherry and silver are the official colors of the university. Because the blazer had "D. H. Lawrence Ranch" embroidered on the pocket over the seal of the University of New Mexico, I assumed he was Don Canon, the staff member I had talked to about the arrangements.

I created my memory walk while the faces and names were fresh in my mind. Except it wasn't a walk, it was a drive across the country. I pictured Benthrop in California, a phony playing at being an intellectual. Winant was in Arizona, on the lookout for illegal aliens who might be headed for Vegas to work in the casinos. Betty was in New Mexico for which I was thankful. Saunders was a tall Texan, and so on. I went over the list several times and wondered if it would work. After all, enchiladas and tacos were a lot easier to remember than a bunch of strangers.

20

Susannah had been meeting the same people I had but in a different sequence, and she joined me as Wron walked away.

"Geez, I can see why things got a little confused. I tried to tell people we were friends and you didn't just pick me up at the Museum like a stray cat, but they weren't listening. Maybe it's because they're dignitaries."

"Well, at least most of them seem friendly, unlike California and Arizona."

"California and Arizona?"

"Benthrop and Winant."

"Oh, your memory walk thing."

Don Canon (West Virginia) came over to welcome us. "I'm sorry the phones are not working. I suppose it's the weather. Also, you need to know the Conference Center is completely non-smoking. If you have to smoke, you'll have to go outside. Be aware there is a steep cliff just to the west of the parking area. There's a guard rail, but it might be covered with snow by now."

"Do the electric lines ever go down in a storm like the phone lines have?"

He shrugged. "I'm not sure."

He was so organized when we spoke about the arrangements that I was surprised by his uncertainty about the electricity. It made me nervous.

Saunders, the retired judge, overheard my questions and told me he read in the brochure he received with his invitation that the Ranch had its own electric generator, so even if the grid went down because of the storm, we wouldn't be affected. He also said he noticed there was plenty of firewood, so at least the big room would be warm although the bedrooms might get a bit cold at night.

Betty joined us, and Susannah seized the opportunity to set the record straight. "Thanks for introducing us to everyone," she said. "I guess I didn't mention that I've known Hubie for... well, it seems forever."

"I know just how you feel. Even though I met him for the first time tonight, he seems like an old friend. It must be a gift he has."

"But I really mean it," Susannah insisted.

"Of course you do. Oh, try some of this bean dip. It's absolutely fabulous."

Susannah shrugged and walked away. All the states were standing around chatting, and California and Arizona (Benthrop and Winant) had returned to the foyer where they were cloistered in conversation, whispering to each other in a conspiratorial manner.

Betty saw me looking in their direction and said, "What a pair!"

"How was Benthrop's talk?" I asked.

"Dreadful. You were wise to skip it. But Winant loved it. They've become inseparable since that talk."

"What do you do, Betty?"

"Mostly charity work. My husband left me a ton of money, and I enjoy giving some of it away." She edged a little closer, "But I'm no angel. I spend quite a lot of it having fun."

I resisted the temptation to ask what kind of fun for fear of where the conversation might lead. She had long lean limbs and a trim waist. I don't know why I thought she was in her mid fifties. As I got a better look at her, I began to think she was closer to my age. O.K., I'm not all that far from fifty myself.

She asked me what my talk would be about, and I told her I was planning to show pictures of old Indian pots and talk about how they were made.

"Benthrop should love your talk. He says white civilization has self-destructed, and we are in the early stages of the next phase in the development of the human psyche where people of color will be in their ascendancy."

"How did that come up in a lecture on Lawrence?"

"He said Lawrence was the harbinger of the end of white supremacy. Why do you suppose he would say that?"

"I have no idea. I don't pretend to understand literature, but from the little bit I've read of Lawrence, I wouldn't have said he was the harbinger of anything unless it was the decline of punctuation."

"I read *Lady Chatterley's Lover*," she volunteered.

"And?"

"It made me think about hiring a gardener."

I laughed and she held out her glass to me. "Vodka rocks," she said and went off to the ladies room.

I fixed her drink and another one for myself. I took a few sips while Betty was gone. She came back refreshed, and I handed her a drink about which the same thing could be said.

Her posture was perfect and her walk graceful. It occurred to me that she was actually probably younger than me.

I was staring at her remarkably taut skin, wide mouth and supple lips. Did I mention her makeup was expertly applied?

She leaned in to me and asked, "Do you know that all the rooms are taken?"

"No, I didn't know that."

"I figured that," she said. "Otherwise, you wouldn't have brought the damsel in distress."

I had just finished my third Old Granddad, which I guess made the last one my great, great granddad, so I wasn't sure who the damsel in distress was. I figured out it was Susannah just as Betty asked me where the damsel was planning to sleep, and I answered "with me" without thinking of how that sounded. Betty kissed me on the cheek, wished me sweet dreams and disappeared.

21

"Hubie, are you asleep?"

"Yes," I replied. I guess it goes without saying that I lied.

"Why?"

"Why? Because I drove for six hours, walked through deep snow for three miles, and drank an entire genealogy of bourbon." Then I remembered something else. "On an empty stomach."

"Me too."

"You didn't drive for six hours or walk through deep snow for three miles."

"I drove the last three miles and those were the most challenging."

"You didn't drink any bourbon."

"I had wine and that was also on an empty stomach."

"O.K.," I relented. "You can be asleep, too."

"I don't want to be asleep, Hubie. I want to ask you something."

I rolled over to face the bed. The floor was hard, but at least I had my 500-thread-count sheets and my own goose-down pillow. Susannah had volunteered to take the floor because it was my room and she was the interloper, but she's taller than I am and came closer to matching the length of the single bed in the tiny room we were occupying, so I insisted that she take the bed. Plus – and I didn't say this to her – I'm at that age where I have to get up at least once in the middle of the night to go to the bathroom, and I didn't want to have to step over her as I headed down the hall.

There were halls on two opposite sides of the large center room, one on the east and one on the west. We were on the west side that had small bedrooms and a communal bathroom at each end of the hall. The east hall had larger rooms with private baths. At the back of the large room to the north was a storage room for tables, chairs, and other equipment on the left and on the right a commercial kitchen with stainless steel preparation tables, a walk-in freezer and a commercial range. There were three entrances into the kitchen, a large passageway from the main room, a smaller passageway from the east hall, and a service entrance on the back wall.

"What do you want to ask me?"

"Why are you here, Hubie?"

"Is that a philosophical question, Suze? Because I'm really too tired to deal with a question like that."

"No, Hubie, it's not a philosophical question. I don't mean why are you here as in 'what is your purpose in life?' I mean why are you in this room when you could be with Betty?"

"Huh?"

"I saw the way you were looking at her there at the end, Hubie."

"That wasn't me staring at her. That was my Old Granddad."

"Come on, Hubie, she's not that old."

"It was a joke, Suze. I don't know how old she is. She seemed to be getting younger as the night wore on, and I remembered an old joke about how women in a bar start to look better as closing time approaches, and I think this was a version of that phenomenon."

"Well, she was obviously coming on to you, Hubie, and I'm just wondering why you didn't react?"

"Umm. Well, see, the thing is, she asked me where you would be sleeping and, uh..."

"Oh, jeez, don't tell me you told her I'd be sleeping with you."

"I didn't mean it the way it came out. I meant that you'd be in the room – like you are now."

"Well, there's another thing we've got to straighten out in the morning. When you explain at the start of your presentation that you sell pots as a business and you're not simply selling off your legacy, maybe you can add that we're just friends."

"I don't know, Suze. Don't you think it would be a little awkward for me to announce out of the blue that we're not sleeping together?"

"Hmm. I see what you mean. If you say we're just friends, everyone will wonder why you said it, and they'll assume just the opposite." She sighed. "Oh well, it doesn't matter what they think. We'll never see them again, and it's not like there's some guy I'm interested in here, so who cares if they think I'm your girlfriend?"

"You didn't like any of the men here?"

"They're all too old, Hubie. I guess donors are usually old. It must take a lifetime to accumulate enough money to give away."

"I think it's more that people don't start thinking about what to do with their money until they get old."

She gave a brief laugh. "You mean when they finally realize they can't take it with them when they go?"

"I think they've known all along they can't take it with them when they go. I suspect what spurs their generosity is the realization of how soon they'll be making the journey. But Glover and Patel aren't very old."

"Glover is married. You've seen his wife on those car ads... but you don't watch television and you don't follow sports. Howard Glover was an All-Pro fullback in the National Football League. After he retired, he came back to New Mexico and started buying car dealerships. His wife is gorgeous, but she's awful on television."

"UNM had a player good enough to play as a pro?"

"He didn't play at UNM. He played at New Mexico State."

"They play football?"

"Not so's you'd notice."

"What about Patel?"

"He is sort of cute. His hair style gives him a sort of geeky look, and his skin is beautiful. His accent is also adorable. How old do you think he is, Hubie?"

"I don't know. Your age, maybe a little older."

"He's probably married. Anyway, remember I vowed not to try so hard? I'm just going to enjoy the weekend and see what happens."

Fateful words, as it turned out.

I waited until Susannah was asleep and tiptoed out of the room with my clothes. I put them on in the empty hall and went outside. I came back in with more clothes from the emergency supply I keep in the Bronco and with the box with the pot in it. I crept silently back into the room, removed the pot from the box and placed it on the desk. Then I put the clothes from the Bronco over the clothes I already had on, three layers in all, a knit hat under the hood of a parka, cotton gloves inside a bigger pair of leather ones, and large snow boots over insulated socks. I placed the box – empty now except for the peanuts – in a backpack, placed my flashlight in my parka and left the building.

22

Forty minutes later I reached the cabin where D. H. Lawrence had lived.

It was up the road where I had spotted tire tracks as we had driven in earlier that night, but the tracks were no longer visible. It took me forty minutes to walk there because the snow was three feet deep, so I had to ease one leg down until it touched ground and then move it around until I found firm footing. Then I'd pull the other leg up out of the snow – no mean feat – and poke it down into the snow, and repeat the process over and over. It was hard work, and I had to stop every few minutes to catch my breath. The good news was that the air wasn't that cold, perhaps in the high twenties, and my top half was sweating under the parka, the coat, and the sweater. Indeed, I unzipped the parka after the first twenty minutes.

The bottom half of me was faring less well. Despite having on long underwear and thick cotton pants, I felt like I was freezing. The snow clung to my legs, and I was becoming numb all the way up to an area where no man ever wants to be numb. The thought of frostbite crossed my mind and I picked up the pace. My top half was sweltering and my bottom half was freezing, but like the man with his head in the refrigerator and his feet in the stove, I was just right on average.

The first thing I saw was the tree. I had read what Lawrence had written about it. "The big pine tree in front of the house, standing still and unconcerned and alive...the overshadowing tree whose green top one never looks at...One goes out of the door and the tree-trunk is there, like a guardian angel. The tree-trunk, the long work table and the fence!"

The tree was failing its role as a guardian. The door to the cabin was unlocked. I stepped inside, switched on my flashlight and looked at a scene from the 1920's. There were two oil lamps and an inexpertly made adobe fireplace, but no oil and no wood, so no light and no heat. There were tin plates, a cast iron skillet, earthenware jugs, and an old cross-saw. The bedsprings were un-upholstered, not because the fabric had rotted away with age but because they used to make bedsprings that way. There were some old black and white photos of Lawrence, Frieda, and The Brett.

I had never heard of The Honorable Dorothy Eugenie Brett until I read *D. H. Lawrence in Taos*. Between his two stays in New Mexico, Lawrence traveled back to England where he spent most of his time disparaging his native country much to the delight of the café crowd he was running with. I have never figured out why intellectuals never like their own countries. At any rate, Lawrence proposed that they all abandon England which was dead anyway in his view and start a utopian society in New Mexico. All his chums thought this a splendid idea while they were having drinks, but in the clear sunshine of the next day, they found excuses to delay. All except The Brett who turned her back on her home and the privileges of the peerage and went to live on the Ranch. D. H. and Frieda lived in the two room cabin I was standing in. The Brett was in a one room cabin not far away. And these were the citizens of utopia, the son of an English coal-miner, a German woman who left her husband and children to marry him, and an English dame.

The Brett was almost deaf and carried a sort of horn that she would hold up to the mouth of anyone who wanted to speak to her. It sounded almost comical when I read about it. Lawrence would propound some grand philosophical thesis in a room full of painters and writers, and The Brett would make the rounds holding the horn in front of each person in turn to hear what response they had to the Great Man's utterance. Of course all conversation had to cease while she did this. She was a frail and shy thing, and it must have been painfully awkward for her to pass round the room with the horn, but she never complained.

The horn was sitting on a shelf to the right of the sink just above some mismatched wooden chairs around a roughhewn table.

Before The Brett came to America, D. H. and Frieda had spent a winter in this cabin with two Danish painters, and I tried to imagine four people holed up inside the small cabin in the sort of winter weather you get at 8,600 feet. I couldn't understand why anyone would voluntarily subject themselves to it, but apparently there was singing and loud arguments about art and life, and a good time was had by all. And they didn't spend all that time in the cabin anyway because they had to spend hours every day gathering enough firewood to keep from freezing to death.

I walked over to a small side table and saw an assortment of things that had belonged to Lawrence, including a typewriter and a fountain pen, the old-fashioned type you filled from a bottle of ink. And underneath the table, in a position that suggested it had been used as a spittoon, was the Taos pot Lawrence had described in his letter to Witter Bynner and I had seen in two photographs, one when Fidelio Duran took it to Lawrence on his arrival in New Mexico and one on the day Lawrence left the state forever. There was something fatalistic about those two pictures closing a circle. I half expected Fidelio Duran's spirit to speak to me. Goose bumps rose on my neck.

Probably just from the cold.

I sat down at the desk and read an original page in Lawrence's own hand. Next to it was a typed poem by Bynner:

There is an island where a man alone,
Alive beyond the selfishness of living,
Knows the whole world around him as his own
Without resenting and without forgiving.

Maybe that explained how they lived in this cabin.

Or maybe not.

I turned the pot upside down and saw 'Fidelio Duran' henscratched into the clay. I nestled the pot down into the Styrofoam peanuts and returned the box to my backpack. In Bynner's words, the pot would be gone "without resenting and without forgiving," because it was obvious that no one among those who were now running the Ranch had the slightest idea of its meaning and value.

23

I arrived back at the Conference Center just before three in the morning.

The storm had not abated, and it took me ten minutes to clear the drifting snow away from the main door so that I could force it open. Once inside, I walked over to the massive fireplace. Only embers remained, but the residual heat felt good. I placed the Duran pot on the hearth and studied it.

Duran was not a skilled potter. The thickness of the wall varied wildly. The burnishing had not been completed. The top rim kilted to one side. Yet there was something charming about the piece, almost as if a child had made it. I'm always happy to grasp an old pot in my felonious fists, but the feeling running through me that cold night was new. So new, in fact, that I couldn't put a name to it. The best description I could come up with was a feeling of well-being, but that didn't quite capture it.

I buried my face in the pot and inhaled deeply. I fancied I smelled the spicy stew Duran had taken to Lawrence as a welcome to a newcomer. In point of fact, the pot was still so cold that had there been skunk jerky in it, I wouldn't have been able to smell it.

I stripped off the clothes I had taken out of the Bronco and went back outside to put them back inside the truck along with the box containing Duran's pot. I locked the truck, re-entered the building, hung my coat and hat on the rack, went to my room, took off my sweater and trousers and climbed into bed in my shorts and tee shirt.

Then I climbed out again because as soon as I began to get warm, I had to go to the bathroom. I traipsed down the hall in my skivvies, used the facility, returned, eased myself back down onto the floor and under the sheet and blanket and fell immediately into a deep sleep.

I dreamed I was in the Iditarod, except in this version there were no dogs and the contestants had to push the sled through the snow for the entire 1150 miles. The dream me didn't want to be in the race, but somehow I was in it and had no choice but to keep trudging forward. A newspaper reporter was walking alongside me on the trail and interviewing me, and he asked me what "Iditarod" meant. I couldn't answer and he laughed at me. Then I was watching the evening news and there was the tape of me looking foolish and swaying back and forth during the interview because that's the way you move when you walk through deep snow. I was rocking back and forth and pushing my sled and starting to feel motion sickness, and the reporter was calling my name, except now it was a girl, and then it was Susannah and she was shaking me and telling me to wake up, and I finally did and was glad to be out of that dream.

"What time is it?"

"I don't know, but it's light. Look at this, Hubie."

I stood up groggily, holding the sheet around me like a sari. Getting up was difficult because the muscles on the inside of my thighs were sore.

Susannah pulled the curtain back from the window, and snow was packed against it to the very top pane.

"Isn't it beautiful, Hubie? I think we should have some Christmas music."

"It's April."

"Well, you have to grab a white Christmas whenever you have the chance. I'm going to ask Maria if she has any eggnog."

"Who's Maria?"

"The caterer. You know, the cute one with the short dark hair."

I added her to my memory drive by placing her in Maryland because of her name. Baltimore, to be exact. It's one of three cities I can name in Maryland, the other two being Annapolis and Frostburg. She didn't look like a midshipman... midshipwoman? And she was way too warm and cute to be in a place called Frostburg.

"The plump girl is in Maryland," I said.

"That's not nice, Hubie."

"What's wrong with Maryland?"

"I meant the 'plump' part."

"I thought it was better than 'fat'."

"She's not fat."

"What is she?"

"Big-boned?"

"Dinosaurs are big boned, Suze. Maria is plump. That doesn't mean she isn't attractive. In fact, she is. And she's not all that plump. I'd say she's 'pleasingly plump'."

"Well, don't say that to her."

"I'm not planning to say anything to her. You're the one who wants the eggnog."

Susannah went off to see Maria and I went off to shower. I was planning a long hot one but got a short cold one instead, and I have to say I was wide awake afterwards despite getting only four hours of sleep. The building was a bit chilly, so after shaving, brushing, and flossing, I donned heavy cotton trousers and a dark green crew neck sweater and hobbled down to the main room where I found Don Canon and complained about the lack of hot water. He said he already knew it was out, but didn't know how to fix it. Since the electricity was working fine, I assumed the water must be heated by some other source, probably propane, and I was hoping a simple change of tanks would solve the problem. But Canon didn't know anything about the water heating system, and I didn't feel like going outside to search for propane tanks.

One thing I did know was that the kitchen must be electric because the smell of coffee made me realize I was famished. Unfortunately, the only food was last night's cheese and crackers along with some overripe fruit. Even the bean dip was gone. A thin young woman about my height with lank brown hair and a long pale face asked me if I wanted coffee, and I avowed that I did.

"I don't think I met you last night," I said as she filled a mug.

"I was off duty," she said tonelessly.

"I guess the leftovers from last night are all we have for breakfast?"

"You'll have to ask the caterer," she said and walked away. It's hard to find good help. I put her in New Jersey. I'm not sure if New Jersey is actually next to Maryland, but it was worth skipping a state to put whatever her name was there.

Maria the caterer came over to ask me how the coffee was and to apologize for the lack of breakfast food. The original plan, she said, had been for her to drive back to Taos and spend the night in her own place and then come back in the morning with the breakfast supplies. I remembered that Betty had told me all the rooms were taken, and I wondered if that was because the caterer had to stay.

"You're lucky they had a room for you," I said.

"They didn't. I had to room with Ms. Shanile." She angled her head and her eyebrows seemed slightly arched. She was definitely plump. But cute. She reminded me of Dolly except she was shorter. And less plump than Dolly in her current incarnation. And, I thought, less moody. Then I felt guilty for the thought. Something was bothering her, and instead of trying to help, I was complaining.

Maria had a round face with a turned up nose, a small mouth, and a slight overbite. Her coarse hair was cut short, revealing small perfectly formed ears. Her clear eyes peered out at me over prominent cheek bones and seemed to be asking a silent question.

I didn't have an answer, silent or otherwise, so I just kept looking at her, a pleasant enough pastime.

"Would you join me for a cup of coffee?" I asked.

She smiled and sat down. She turned over a mug, and the girl who had filled my mug came and filled Maria's then walked away sullenly.

"I guess she's not expecting a tip," I speculated out loud.

Maria laughed. Then she said good help is hard to find, and I told her I'd had the same thought, and we both laughed. Then we fell silent and she gave me that sort of expectant look again. I liked that look. She looked attractive looking that look. But it also made me a little apprehensive because I didn't know what it meant.

"We had a back-up plan," she said.

"Huh?"

"In case you came to the room."

I must have had a blank stare.

"Ms. Shanile came to me while you were freshening her drink last night and said you might come to the room, and if you did, I was to take your room."

"Oh."

"But you didn't come."

"No."

Her fawn skin looked clear and fresh-scrubbed. There was no hint of make-up except for what I thought was lip gloss. Then she ran her tongue over her lips, and I decided their sheen was natural. Her head was canted again, her mouth ever so slightly ajar, perhaps because of the overbite.

"Why?" she said.

"Why?"

"Yes, why?"

"Why what?"

"Why didn't you come to Ms. Shanile's room?"

"Uh..."

"Am I being too forward?"

I thought she was, in fact, but I didn't want to say so. I liked her and I liked talking to her, and I didn't want to pull the plug on our conversation.

"It's not that," I said, fumbling for words. "It's that I'm not really sure what the answer is. I mean, she didn't actually ask me to come to her room."

She smiled at me. "Ladies don't ask gentlemen to their rooms."

"Oh."

"But they might signal that you would be welcome."

"Um."

"Did you pick up any signals from Ms. Shanile?"

"Well, um, I'm not certain."

"Ms. Shanile thought you had picked up the signals. That's why she asked me if I would mind moving to your room. But when she came to the room, she said you were sleeping with that young woman you picked up at the Rogers Museum, so we girls would just have to enjoy a slumber party without men unless I could find one. She's a funny lady. Nice, too."

"She is," I agreed. "Listen, I'm glad you brought this up because the whole thing is a big misunderstanding. The girl's name is Susannah Inchaustigui, and I didn't pick her up at the Museum. She rode up from Albuquerque with me. She and I have been friends for several years. We had to share a room because there was no place else for her to sleep, but we're just friends."

Maria called New Jersey over – her name turned out to be Adele – and asked her to get us some more coffee. She did so, but it was clear she considered it an imposition.

Maria observed that Susannah must be Basque because of her last name, and I said she was correct, and she asked me if I were Basque, and I said I wasn't. She asked me what I was, and I said American, and she laughed. Then she asked me if I knew what she was.

The answer, from my point of view, was that she too was American, but I knew that wasn't what she meant, and I didn't want to make a boor of myself by getting into a debate about how we divide ourselves into races, tribes and clans, and why I think that obscures the most basic truth about the human species; namely, that any human being, no matter his or her genetics, can belong to any culture.

In fact, I have a list of beliefs I call Schuze' Anthropological Premises, abbreviated SAP, which is what some of my cynical friends say you have to be to believe them. That any human can practice any culture is SAP #1.

In a recent interview, Scott Simon, the National Public Radio host, was talking about the two daughters he and his wife adopted in China. A caller inquired whether they felt guilty taking the girls out of their culture. Simon replied that they were better off with him in a good home than in an orphanage in China. A good answer. But a better one would have been that he and his wife didn't take the girls out of their culture because *infants do not have a culture.*

You aren't born with a culture. You learn it. The Simon girls will be part of American culture because this is where they will be raised. They will not be adept at using chopsticks simply because they were born to a woman in China. If they start learning Chinese in college, it will be just as difficult for them as it would be for any other native English speaker. Your skin color and eye shape do not determine your culture.

Am I ranting? Well, I certainly didn't want to do that to Maria, so I studied her looks again. My original assessment had not changed - she was plump. I would guess maybe a hundred and forty pounds on a 5' 2" frame, but none of it flabby. She was definitely pleasingly plump. She didn't look like a pueblo Indian. I cringe when I say or think things like that, but if you decide to play the game, you have to play it by the rules that exist. She was not Hispanic despite her name, so by a process of elimination, I had a pretty good guess to make.

"You might be a *Jicarilla* Apache," I said.

She gave me a big smile. "Why do you say 'might'?"

"Well," I said hesitatingly, "you're kind of..."

"Short? That's because my mother was a Navaho."

"You don't mind me saying you're short?"

"Why should I? It's true. You're pretty short yourself."

"That's also true."

"You know much about the *Jicarilla*?"

"Not much," I admitted. The *Jicarilla* make great baskets, but I sell pots, so my dealings are mostly with the pueblo tribes.

"Would you like to know more?"

I hesitated while I worked up a little nerve and figured out the best wording. Then I said, "Are you sending me signals?" I was hoping she was. I had a strong desire to squeeze her just to see if she was as firm as she appeared.

She smiled and excused herself because Carla Glain had arrived and was standing next to our table asking about breakfast. After Maria went to find Adele the Serving Wench, Carla plopped down at my table without being invited and said, "I see you're a liar and a phony like most men."

"Good morning," I replied. Talking to Maria had put me in a great mood. She was perky, bright, and fun. I wasn't going to let Carla Glain rain on my parade.

"You want to know why you're a phony?"

"Not really. I just want to enjoy my coffee." Then I added, "How are things in Alabama?"

"You're a phony," she said, ignoring both my response and frivolous comment, "because you pretended last night to be a feminist when you agreed with me that women have been excluded from the workplace and marginalized economically by being limited to handicrafts."

"I do believe that."

"Maybe, but you are no feminist. There you were making a fool of yourself staring at Betty Shanile all evening, and then when a young girl is suddenly available, you drop the mature woman without so much as a backwards glance."

How did I get into this conversation? I didn't want to make a scene. I was here to entertain the dignitaries. I decided not to be provoked.

"The young girl is a friend of mine. We shared a room only because there was no other place for her to sleep."

"Humph. Are you also going to deny that you were flirting with Betty Shanile?"

"I thought it was the other way around," said Maria, who had just walked up to our table with a carafe of steaming coffee. "Can I pour you some coffee?"

"I'm not thirsty," said Glain, and she got up and walked away.

"Thanks for rescuing me," I said.

Maria smiled and started making the rounds of the other tables where everyone had gathered except for Betty, Charles Winant the fundamentalist anti-gambling boor, Agatha Cruz the disheveled older lady, and Fred Rich, the fast food guy whom I had located as a food hawker in New Orleans.

Susannah and Srinivasa Patel asked me if I needed help setting up my presentation. I said I did, and we picked out the west wall for a screen and arranged some chairs facing it at a comfortable distance. We dragged one of the tables into position and placed the laptop and projector on it. Srini plugged in the equipment and brought up the slide show for me. The first slide was on the wall but looked slightly fuzzy, so Susannah adjusted the focus on the projector. I looked at the introductory slide and suddenly became nervous.

I went to my room and brought out the Anasazi pot, placed it on the table next to the projector, and draped a tablecloth over it. I was hoping to auction it off, but that seemed somehow less plausible now than it had when Susannah had first suggested it. It also seemed less important in light of the Duran pot sitting in the Bronco.

I sat down behind the table and tried to relax. I thought about taking the table cloth off the pot and draping it over myself.

24

The group drifted over shortly after ten. Everyone was present except for the four who had missed breakfast: Betty Shanile, Charles Winant, Agatha Cruz, and Fred Rich. All the others took seats except the two staffers, Don Canon who remained standing behind the last row of chairs and Adele the Serving Wench who went off to do her chores. Maria asked if she could see the presentation, and I told her she could and was glad she wanted to. Charles Winant came in saying he had overslept, and then Betty made her first appearance of the day just as I picked up the device that controls the projector, and she took a seat in the front next to Carl Wron.

I took a deep breath and started talking about how the Native Americans made pots before the arrival of the Europeans. I talked a little about clays and firings, and a little more about pigments, glazes, and slips, but mostly I talked about designs. I showed a variety of pots from four different pueblos – Zia, Acoma, Santo Domingo, and Picuris. Many of the other pueblos have made great pottery, but I wanted to keep it simple and brief.

I then talked about a process known as burnishing, a method of polishing a pot by rubbing it with a smooth bone. I noted that Native Americans were using this technique centuries before Europeans arrived, and I explained that the burnishing process filled the small pores in dried clay with particles and therefore made the pots less permeable so that they held liquids better. But burnishing also has an aesthetic affect because it orients all the particles in one direction and creates a sort of mirrored surface. I showed several slides of burnished pots and pot fragments found in New Mexico and dating back to the time of Christ.

Then I reminded them that Christ lived under the Roman Empire, and I showed them some pictures of Roman pots that had been burnished in exactly the same manner as the pots in New Mexico. The effect was as dramatic as I had hoped and led me into my closing observation.

"The widespread view today," I began, "is that Europeans started colonizing the world about five-hundred years ago and subjected almost all the world's indigenous peoples to evils ranging from forced religious conversion, to destruction of their languages, to outright genocide. That view is mostly correct, but it is rarely seen in the wider context. So think about this. The most proficient colonizer in human history was the United Kingdom. At one time, they controlled almost all of North America, Australia, New Zealand, most of the Indian subcontinent, a good deal of Africa, most of the Middle East, and various islands in every ocean. It was true that the sun never set on the British Empire. Yet in 1066, the British Isles themselves were invaded and conquered, and the way of life of the then indigenous people forcibly changed forever. At about the same time here in New Mexico, the Anasazi were building cliff dwellings. Why? To protect themselves from raiding nomadic tribes who would kill some of them and take others of them slaves. My point is that the history of the human race is the history of thousands of tribes over thousands of years fighting, conquering, and mistreating those who are from a different tribe."

I finished by saying, "Winston Churchill once said, 'History will be kind to us. We know this, for we shall write it.' History is written by the victors. But where is the historian who will recognize that we are all the victors and we are all the vanquished, and which group we belong to depends on the time and place you happen to be talking about? I think we need to end this destructive cycle, and perhaps the first step is to start emphasizing the many things we all have in common as human beings and start de-emphasizing the few differences that lead to strife. Well, let me take off my orator's hat and go back to being a potter, which is probably more in keeping with my character, and let me show you a thing of beauty."

I lifted the tablecloth off the pot with a flourish, and there was a blood curdling scream.

25

The first thing that crossed my mind was that someone was horrified by the sight of the pot.

Which just goes to show that your first thoughts are not always your most rational ones.

The scream had come from down the east hallway, and we all rushed in its direction. The door to one of the guest rooms was open, and through it I could see Adele with her hands curled up against her mouth, staring into the bathroom. As we crowded around her and looked in, I saw Fred Rich's naked body floating in the bathtub. An electrical cord stretched from an outlet above the lavatory over the edge of the tub, into the water, and under Rich's body.

Because the table I was standing by during my presentation was nearer to the east hall than were the chairs, I got to Rich's room quickly despite my sore thighs. Only Don Canon beat me there, and he was younger and probably didn't have sore legs.

He turned to the others coming in and said – rather idiotically, I thought – "is anyone here a doctor?"

"I'm a doctor," said Benthrop, another example of your first thoughts not being your best.

Everyone stared at him.

"Oh. I suppose you want a medical doctor," he said lamely.

Charles Winant elbowed his way past Canon, Adele and me and, looking down into the tub, announced, "The Lord has taken Fred Rich."

For some reason, the thought that came first to my mind was that Fred Rich wouldn't be flipping any more burgers. At least I had the good sense not to voice that thought.

Others started to creep forward, but Carl Wron said, "You ladies may not want to see this," and tried to shoo them out.

Susannah, never squeamish about such things, came forward with Srini and peeked in. Srini kept repeating, "Oh, my, oh, my."

Maria Salazar and Betty Shanile heeded Carl Wron's suggestion and went back to the main room. Benthrop had already left, perhaps embarrassed by his remark about being a doctor. Adele seemed almost catatonic. Canon took her by the arm and led her away. Carla Glain looked in at Rich's body, showed no reaction, and left.

Howard Glover unplugged the electric cord and reached down into the water to feel for a pulse. He looked up at us and shook his head. "We should get him out of here," he said.

"I don't think so," said Teodoro Vasquez, the lobbyist. "I think we should wait for the authorities and not disturb anything."

Robert Saunders joined the crowd at the door to the bathroom and said, "The authorities might be days getting in here. We can't leave a dead body floating in a tub. It's not hygienic."

"You got a point," said Glover.

"We could call the authorities. They could be here in hours," said Vasquez.

"Call them how?" asked Saunders. "The land lines are down and we're out of cell phone range."

We all looked at each other, but no one had anything to say. It had been obvious all morning that we were stranded by the blizzard, but no one had talked about it. Now that we had a corpse in our midst, we needed to assess our situation.

Saunders must have been having the same thoughts. He said in his judicial voice, "Let's all go back to the main room and discuss this."

"What about the body?" asked Glover.

"It won't hurt to leave it for an hour until we decide what we need to do."

No one moved for a moment. Then Glover shrugged and walked out and everyone followed. I was the last one out, and I peeked into Rich's toiletry bag beside the lavatory as I left.

26

Robert Saunders said in an authoritative voice, "May I have everyone's attention please. As you know, Mr. Rich is dead. The normal course of action would be to call the police who would then handle calling the coroner if necessary, arranging to have the body removed, and notifying the next of kin. Unfortunately, that option is not available to us. The phone lines are down, and we're out of range of any cell phone towers. Mr. Canon, is there by any chance some other sort of communication option for emergency purposes? Do you have a radio phone, a satellite phone, or anything of that nature?"

Canon shook his head.

"Then I think the first order of business is to get somebody down the mountain to contact the police. How far is it to the main road?"

Canon said, "I don't know exactly."

"It's three miles," I said.

"How do you know that?" asked Saunders.

"Because I was the last one to come up here last night and the road was covered with snow. I had to walk in front of my vehicle while Susannah drove because I didn't know if there were culverts, wash-outs, or other hazards. I checked the odometer when I got out to start walking and when we arrived. It was exactly three miles."

"Someone will need to walk back to the road with a cell phone and call the police."

"I'm not sure that's possible," I said. "I'm also not sure it's advisable."

"Surely someone can walk three miles even in the snow," offered Teodoro Vasquez.

"I'll go," Glover volunteered.

Everyone was anxious to accept his offer and there were expressions of thanks and good luck being offered when I cut in.

"Suppose he's not back in seven or eight hours," I posed. "What are we going to do then?"

"I'll be back long before that," said Glover.

"I'm sure you think so. But suppose you aren't. Do we send a search party to find you? It will be dark by then. Then what if they don't come back?"

"Good heavens, Hubie," said Betty, "this isn't some B-grade horror movie. Mr. Glover is a big strong man. I'm sure he can walk three miles through the snow."

"What harm can it do just to run a test?" I asked.

"Better safe than sorry," added Srini.

Glover stood up and said he didn't mind doing a test just to satisfy some of us, and he went to his room and returned in coat, hat, and boots.

"I'll go a hundred yards and back, and you time it," he said, looking at me with what I thought was an expression of disdain.

"How will you know when you've gone a hundred yards?"

"I spent most of my life on football fields. I know how long a hundred yards is."

Susannah said, "I don't remember any running back from New Mexico State ever going a hundred yards."

Glover glared at her. He opened the front door and there was a collective gasp. The snow was all the way to the top of the doorway. He looked back at us, then turned to the snow, put his head down, and plowed into it. After he had gone a few steps, snow tumbled down into the space he had created, and we could see that the snow around the door was a drift. He pushed most of it aside. The depth of the snow away from the building was about four feet. Glover waved then started off.

He returned eight minutes later. After he removed his outdoor gear, I noted to the group that since it took him eight minutes to cover 200 yards, that meant it would take approximately four hours to get to the road and back.

Glain, speaking in a rapid monotone, said, "A mile is 1760 yards. Divide that by the 200 yards he traveled and you get 8.8. Multiply that by the eight minutes it took him, and you get 70.4 minutes. So it would take him one hour, ten minutes, and 24 seconds for each mile."

There was a moment of complete silence while everyone gaped at her.

Susannah asked, "How did you do that?"

Glain replied, "Some women can do math, Missy," and Susannah shot back, "And most can do manners."

Saunders held up a hand and said, "Let's not squabble. If Ms. Glain is correct—"

"I am correct," said Glain.

Saunders continued, "That means it would take him three and a half hours to reach the road."

Glover was wearing a grim expression. "Longer," he said. "I couldn't keep up that pace for long. I suspect it would be closer to five hours."

"So let's say it took five hours," said Saunders. "It's already noon. If he got down there and couldn't make contact, it would take him another five to come back—"

"Longer," said Glover, "I'd be coming up hill."

"Why do you think he might not make contact?" Vasquez asked Saunders.

"Because we don't know where the nearest cell phone towers are. If the nearest tower is in Taos, you might have to go down the main road towards town before getting in range."

Betty asked how far that would be.

No one knew. Then Srini hesitantly said he knew a little about cell phone technology.

"So how close do we have to be to a tower to get reception?" Saunders asked him.

"It's not a matter of how close. Cell phone signals are line of sight. On flat terrain, you might reach thirty miles, but in these mountains, who knows?"

"So if the nearest tower is in Taos, someone would have to walk far enough to be within sight of it?"

"Exactly."

"That ain't gonna happen until the road is plowed," said Glover.

"Surely the main highway has been plowed by now," said Benthrop.

"I doubt it," said Wron. "It's still snowing. They usually wait until it stops."

"But they can't just leave us up here!" said Benthrop, his voice rising.

"I'm not worried," said Winant. "I leave everything to the Lord."

"I hope he does take-out," said Glain. "I'm starving."

"Blasphemer!" shouted Winant.

Saunders said that Glain had a point, and he asked Maria about the food supply. She said there was still a small amount of the cheese and crackers she had brought, and she had checked the cupboards and found corn oil, flour, salt, pepper, mustard, ketchup, sugar, tea, and coffee. The refrigerator had butter, pickles, mayonnaise, and two quarts of coffee creamer, and the freezer was empty except for half an elk carcass.

"We'll starve to death!" cried Benthrop.

"The Lord will provide," countered Winant. I sensed the bindings on their new friendship were unraveling.

"We better get that elk out and start carving it," said Wron. He nodded to Glover and the two of them headed towards the kitchen.

"Wait just a minute," said Saunders, and he turned to me. "Mr. Schuze, when you said you weren't sure it would be possible for someone to walk to the road, you also added you didn't think it was advisable. Why did you say that?"

It was time for me to say it. "Because Fred Rich was murdered."

27

I now had their undivided attention.

"That's utter nonsense," said Winant. "The man killed himself, a mortal sin that he will pay for throughout eternity."

"Why do you say that?" asked Glover.

"Because our lives are not our own. Only God can—"

"I'm not interested in your preaching, Winant. I want to know why you think Rich killed himself." His tone caused Winant to recoil.

"He dropped his electric shaver in the water to electrocute himself. I saw you unplug it before you reached in the water to check his pulse."

Glover nodded. "I thought you might say that. I pulled the plug because I didn't know what it was attached to, and I don't take unnecessary chances. When I lifted his arm, I saw it was the shaver, and I wondered what it was doing in there, but I knew it didn't electrocute him."

"Why couldn't an electric shaver electrocute him?" asked Betty.

"Because it runs on twelve volts, not enough to electrocute a bug."

"But the cord was plugged into a socket."

"Yes, but the box on the plug is a transformer that lowers the voltage. The wire to the shaver is only twelve volts."

"But maybe he didn't know that. I certainly didn't, and evidently Winant didn't know that either."

Glover furrowed his brow. "You saying he threw the shaver in the tub trying to electrocute himself?"

"It could happen."

"I suppose it could. But it still wouldn't kill him, so how did he die?"

All eyes turned to me. I said I didn't know how he died, and Benthrop asked me in his best indignant tone why I had said Rich was murdered if I didn't know how he had died.

"Glover wondered why the shaver was in the tub. I did too. There's only one good explanation I can think of. I think the murderer, like Betty and Charles, didn't know the shaver was only twelve volts, and he threw it in after he killed Rich in order to make it look like a suicide."

"That's it?" said Benthrop. "That's your logic? No wonder you gave us that lame rationalization for European hegemony this morning. Your brain must be fried from breathing too many glazing fumes."

"How else would the shaver get into the tub?" I asked.

"Maybe," said Saunders, "he slipped while he was shaving and fell into the tub with the shaver in his hand."

Glover pointed out that the mirror and lavatory were four feet away from the tub, and there was no way you could fall from there and end up completely in the tub. "Maybe he had already finished his bath, dried off with the towel, went over to drain the water out, slipped at that point and still had the shaver in his hand," said Saunders.

"That's the second reason why I think he was murdered," I said. "He didn't take a bath." I looked around at the group. "Any of you have hot water this morning?" They all shook their heads. "When you discover there's no hot water, you either take a very quick shower or just a sponge bath. Nobody would submerge himself in an icy bath."

"Maybe he was in that polar bear club," said Susannah. She and I started to laugh but stifled it when we saw the looks we were getting from the others.

"A tub full of icy water. A shaver in the tub. I don't say it adds up to murder," said Saunders, "but it does make you wonder."

"There's something else, isn't there?" Glover asked me.

"There is," I said. "Rich shaved with a blade."

28

Maria gave each of us a paper plate with two pieces of cheese, three crackers, and a piece of fruit, telling us we needed to ration the remaining food. Just the mention of the word 'ration' made me hungry.

I had explained that I saw shaving nicks on Rich that could be made only by a regular razor and that his toiletry bag contained disposable razors, shaving cream, and a septic pencil. The topic had been roundly discussed by the group and had divided us into two factions. Those who favored my murder theory included Susannah (whether out of reason or out of loyalty I can't say), Betty Shanile, Srinivasa Patel, Robert Saunders, Howard Glover, and Carl Wron.

Those who thought it possible that Rich used both an electric shaver and a disposable razor and that the murder theory was far-fetched included Charles Winant, Teodoro Vasquez, Don Canon, and Chauncey Benthrop.

Carla Glain said she had no opinion on the matter and didn't really care whether Rich had been murdered, committed suicide, or died of natural causes. Maria Salazar and Adele the Serving Wench were preparing the food during this discussion, so we didn't know where they stood.

One thing everyone finally agreed on was that we were going to be stuck here for a while, and we had to move Rich's body, so despite some expressions of disgust and even horror, Howard Glover lifted the body out of the tub, Carl Wron draped a sheet over it, and Glover deposited it in the walk-in freezer. During this process, they discovered a nasty discolored spot on the back of Rich's head. The adherents of my murder theory took this as evidence of a fatal blow. The skeptics thought Rich must have hit his head when he fell into the tub.

Agatha Cruz had still not emerged from her room, and I was beginning to worry about her, so I asked Don if maybe we should check on her, and he dispatched Adele the Serving Wench to do so.

"Typical," said Carla Glain. "Ask a man to do something and he immediately assigns the work to a woman."

Don wisely refrained from being drawn into debate.

After depositing Fred Rich in the walk-in freezer, Carl Wron and Howard Glover dragged the elk carcass outside through the service entrance at the back of the kitchen and were doing God knows what to it. It wasn't really a carcass as Maria had described it, more of a side of beef except instead of the two legs being cut off at the joint as they are in a normal butchering operation, they were intact. And of course it wasn't a side of beef because it was elk. Maria knew that from the hooves.

Then we heard an engine start up, and I wondered if someone was foolish enough to try to drive away through the snow. The engine revved up and then slowed down and then revved up again. Maria could see us all looking perplexed, so she explained that Carl had a chainsaw in his pickup, and he and Howard were using it to cut up the elk. If that didn't work, they had taken along an ax as well. When the noise of the chainsaw finally stopped, I heard a series of muffled thuds. That went on for about half an hour while I tried without success not to picture what a side of elk looks like after being worked over with a chainsaw and an ax.

My interest in dinner lessened considerably.

Cruz finally emerged looking somewhat the worse for wear. Her make-up was even worse than when I had met her last night. There was powder on her blouse. Her glasses were so greasy that I wondered how she could see. But her hair was almost perfect. Have you ever noticed the obsession older ladies seem to have with their hair? Hers was not quite blue, but it was a shade of silver tending in that direction.

We were scattered around the main room, and everyone looked up and fell silent when she entered. She seemed self-conscious as the center of attention and eased down into a chair at the nearest table.

"Adele told me about poor Mr. Rich," she said to no one in particular.

I took a glass of water to her and sat down across the table from her. "Did you know Mr. Rich before you came to this event?"

She shook her head.

"What brought you here?"

"I'm a university donor."

"So I understand. But why did you accept their invitation for a weekend at the Ranch?"

She looked up at me as if it were an unusual or difficult question. "I didn't have anything else to do."

She looked like one of those ladies you read about from time to time who wear old clothes, live in a one-room apartment amidst stacks of neatly folded grocery bags, and leave a million dollars to their cats when they die.

She declined my offer to get her some food, and I went to my room to get some rest. Last night's hike through the snow and the lack of sleep were getting to me. I needed a nap.

I was just reclining when Susannah came in. I offered her the bed, but she said she didn't come in to rest. She wanted to talk to me.

"Did she admit anything?" she asked.

"Did who admit anything?"

"Agatha Cruz. She has to be the prime suspect, Hubie."

"How do you figure that?"

"She's the only one without an alibi. All the rest of us were at your lecture. So the only one who could have clobbered Rich from behind with a blunt instrument was Agatha Cruz."

"You're forgetting Adele the Serving Wench. She wasn't at the lecture either."

"It's not nice to call her a wench, Hubie. I'm a waitperson, and I wouldn't want to be called a wench."

"'Wench' isn't a description of her job, Suze. It's a description of how she does it."

"Oh. Well, she couldn't have murdered Rich because the person who finds the body is never the murderer unless it's a locked-room mystery, and Rich wasn't locked in his room alone."

Susannah often befuddles me but in an enjoyable way, if that makes any sense. So I asked why the person who discovers the body can be the murderer in a locked-room mystery.

"Not in all of them. Just in one particular type. There are more solutions than you might think. There are the ones where the murderer was in the room all along except cleverly hidden. There's the old standby of using a wire or a magnet or something to lock the door from the outside so that when the victim is found it appears he had locked himself in. There's the discovery of a secret passage into the room." She shook her head in disgust. "I never liked those, Hubie. It seems like cheating to throw in another way into a locked room. But the best solutions are more creative, and one of those is that the victim in the locked room isn't really dead. The people who find him break down the door and see him on the floor. But what they don't know is he isn't dead – he's just unconscious. One member of the group – maybe even a policeman – bends over the victim as if to check what happened and kills him, maybe with a quick injection the others don't see."

I wondered if that could have been the case with Fred Rich. Was he alive when we heard the scream? Don Canon got there first, but he didn't do it because I was right behind him and he didn't touch Rich or the tub, and after that there were so many people around that I didn't see how one of them... But Howard Glover had reached into the water.

Could he have reached under an unconscious Fred Rich and delivered a fatal blow? He's a big, powerful football player, and...

And then I came to my senses and said, "I've forgotten what this has to do with Fred Rich."

"His room wasn't locked," she reminded me.

"Oh, right. Well, it doesn't matter anyway because no one has an alibi."

"But we were all at your lecture."

"We were at the lecture when he was *found*, Suze. But we don't know where we were when he was killed because we don't know when that was."

"But it has to be just before he was found, doesn't it?"

"He had that room by himself. He could have been killed anytime after we all turned in last night. He was discovered during my lecture only because that was when Adele the Serv... that was when Adele was making her rounds cleaning the rooms."

"Maybe we shouldn't have put him in the freezer, Hubie. Now the police won't be able to establish the time of death."

I glanced at her and waited.

"Oh, right," she said. "He was found in a tub of icy water, so it doesn't matter." Then she shivered. "Do you think we're in any danger, Hubie?"

"I don't see why we should be. Whoever killed Fred Rich must have had a reason. We don't have any connection to anyone here, so I don't think we have any reason to be worried."

"Good, because I would really hate to be the next victim."

"There won't be a next victim, Suze. Somebody wanted Fred Rich dead, and he killed him. There's no reason for him to kill anyone else."

"Maybe there was a witness. That's pretty common, Hubie, for a witness to be the second victim."

"If there was a witness, I'm sure he would have come forward immediately."

"Not if he were blackmailing the murderer."

I told her she was reading too many murder mysteries and that I really needed a nap. She returned to the big room and I went to sleep.

29

I enjoyed a sound sleep, pushed no sleds, and awoke to a heavenly scent wafting from the kitchen.

I visited the bathroom down the hall to give my face an icy wash and my teeth an icy brush and went into the main room where the table was laid for cocktails. Maria had evidently brought enough liquor for the entire weekend her first trip (that had now turned out to be her only trip) and everyone was drinking wine except for Betty who was drinking vodka. I wondered what had happened to the bottle of Old Granddad from last night. It had been half full after my third drink, but I was glad to see a new bottle on the table. Although starvation remained a threat, sobriety did not.

I poured myself a generous libation and made a toast to the bourbons. The ones from Kentucky, not the ones from Spain. I asked Susannah if she knew what was cooking. She said it was elk, and images of chainsaws and axes popped up on my mental screen, but she told me we were in for a great treat because she had already tasted the sauce.

"Maria asked all the women to help her prepare supper, but Agatha said she didn't know how to cook and was still feeling under the weather, Adele must have been off duty and Carla complained that Maria didn't ask the men, and that left Betty and me as assistants. The guys did a great job of cutting out the rib roast even though the meat was frozen, and Maria put it in the oven on a wire rack over a cookie sheet at low temperature. Then guess what, Hubie. We all put on our warm clothes and went out into the woods and picked juniper berries."

"Why," I asked, "Was someone suffering from respiratory problems?"

"No. We wanted the juniper berries for cooking not for medicine. Did you know that juniper berries are the main flavor in sauerbraten?"

"I've never eaten sauerbraten that I'm aware of."

"How could you eat anything without being aware of it? Anyway, after the elk had been roasting a couple of hours, Maria melted a whole pound of butter in a giant pan and started stirring flour in it. Then when all the flour and butter had been combined and stirred like crazy, she poured in the coffee creamer while we stirred so it wouldn't lump up. Then she poured the drippings from the cookie sheet into the big pan and we stirred some more. Wow, I never knew how much stirring you have to do. Then guess what she added."

"The juniper berries?"

"Right, but first she put them in a frying pan with no oil or water or anything and heated them up. She showed us how to move the pan around so that all those little purple berries just kept rolling around and didn't stick to the pan. You should have smelled the scent those berries gave off. It was sweet and sort of acidy at the same time and it sort of smelled like gin except a lot better because I don't like gin and neither do you, so maybe what it smelled like was the woods on a fresh spring day."

I nodded in understanding.

"Then – wait 'til you hear this – she poured about a cup of bourbon into the frying pan and set it on fire. The flames shot up and we all jumped back – are my eyebrows singed?"

I told her they weren't. And I knew what had happened to the rest of the first bottle of Old Granddad.

"When the flames died down, we poured the juniper berries into the big pan and started stirring again. It started to thicken too much, so she added a little water, and we stirred some more. Then she poured it through a strainer. There were lumps, Hubie. I hate to say it, as much as we stirred, but there were lumps. But they're all gone now. Then she turned the oven way up to finish cooking the meat and make sure the outside has a nice crust and the inside is pink and juicy. Which I'm sure is exactly how it came out, but we can't eat it now because it's resting. Did you know meat has to rest after it gets cooked?"

I told her if she had been roasted in an oven for four hours, she'd probably need to rest afterwards, too, and she laughed. I said I'd never seen her so excited about cooking, and she said cooking with Maria had given her a new attitude about it, and now she understood why I like to cook.

I finished my first bourbon and had just helped myself to a second when Betty and Maria brought in the roast because it took two people to carry it. The ribs protruded from the meat, and I guess it would have been a standing rib roast except for the fact that it was too big to stand up, so maybe it was a reclining rib roast. Whatever it was, it looked and smelled delicious. Glover was enlisted to do the carving, and he slid a long knife with a serrated blade between the ribs, revealing a hot juicy cross section of the loin with each rib. We filed through cafeteria style, and he placed one slice on each plate. They were caveman proportions, and some of the women said they couldn't eat that much, but he just smiled and said that was how he carved it.

Maria stood to Glover's right and drizzled the sauce over the meat. There was no salad. No vegetables. No sides of any kind, not even one of those little red crabapple rings. It was just meat and gravy. And no one complained.

As we had witnessed the meat being carried in and gone through the line commenting on how good it looked and how delicious it smelled, it seemed to me that a kind of camaraderie was developing among us. Some of it may have been just being stuck together, the misery loves company thing, and some of it may have been that we were drinking, but I think a lot of it was the food and the realization that Maria and Betty and Susannah had done something special for us under unlikely and trying conditions.

Susannah was seated opposite me at one of the square tables with a chair on each side, and we resisted the temptation to dig in. When everyone had been served, the other two members of the kitchen brigade came to our table, Betty to my right and Maria to my left.

There had been a lot of chit chat and laughter, but when we all got seated and started eating, the room fell silent except for the clinking of forks and knives. Hunger is said to be the best sauce, but the juniper sauce was even better, and the elk was cooked to perfection. I'm not a fan of game. I don't like venison or antelope. But elk is not gamey at all. It's tender, juicy, and lean. And this was the best elk I had ever tasted, maybe the best meat I had ever tasted. I was giving serious consideration to asking Maria to marry me, but that would have been awkward with Betty sitting there. Besides, Betty was also attractive and nice and closer to my age. But could she cook? Then I remembered Dolly, and decided not to think about women.

Which immediately proved impossible to do when someone started rubbing a foot playfully against my shins. I couldn't tell if it was Betty or Maria or even Susannah trying to play a trick on me. I didn't know where to look, so I pretended nothing was happening.

Maria noticed the ice had melted in my drink and said she would get me some more from the freezer. When she headed for the kitchen, I figured if the footsy stopped, I would know it had been her, and if not, it was Betty. Or Susannah in a mischievous mood. All the others had finished their meals, pushed back from their tables, and were sitting in silent contentment. A massive log was burning down in the fireplace, and I figured between the warmth on our faces and the meat in our tummies, we would soon all be snoozing.

If we had, the day's second blood-curdling scream would have awakened us.

30

This time it came from the kitchen. We rushed in to see Maria holding open the door to the walk-in freezer and staring in at a naked, frost-covered Charles Winant.

"Jesus," said Susannah, "he's frozen to death."

"Schuze was right," cried Benthrop. "Fred Rich was murdered. And now Charles Winant. Someone is trying to kill us all. We can't just sit around while he picks us off one by one. We need to do something *now*." He looked to Glover with pleading eyes.

"We don't know that Winant was murdered," said Glover.

"Of course we do!" screeched Benthrop. "Do you think he went into the freezer and took all his clothes off as a bizarre means of suicide? Whoever killed him must have stripped his clothes off so he'd freeze to death faster."

"Then why wouldn't Winant have put his clothes back on after the killer left him in the freezer?"

That stumped Benthrop, but not for long. He looked at each of us for suggestions or support, but none was forthcoming. Finally he turned back to Glover. "Maybe he was already dead."

"Then why would the killer bother to remove Winant's clothes?"

"I don't know. But someone took his clothes off."

"No," said Carla Glain, "he probably took them off himself."

She was speaking from behind the crowd at the door of the freezer, and everyone turned to look at her.

"It's called paradoxical undressing," she said clinically. "Many homeless people who freeze to death have been mistakenly identified as victims of sexual assault because they were found with their clothes off. When your temperature drops down into the mid-eighties, your body tries to save itself by quickly dilating the blood vessels near the body's surface, and that creates a sensation of extreme heat against the skin. The freezing victim isn't thinking too clearly anyway, and they strip off their clothes because they feel like their skin is burning."

"How do you know about this?" asked Saunders.

"I work for the Albuquerque chapter of Justice Now, a victim advocacy group. We learned about paradoxical undressing at a conference on homelessness."

"You people are all missing the point," said Benthrop. His brow was damp and there were red splotches on his face. I just hoped he wasn't about to undress himself paradoxically. "Instead of wasting time trying to figure out exactly how Winant died, we should be getting ready to get out of here."

"And how do you propose we do that?" asked Saunders.

"We should all put on the warmest clothing we have and then just march down the mountain together. It may be a long walk, but if we go as a group we can make it."

"You're wrong," said Glover. "I had to work like a dog just to go two-hundred yards." He looked around at the group. "Most of you don't have the strength or stamina to fight through deep snow for an hour, much less for ten or twenty hours or even longer. What do we do when you run out of gas? Leave you in the snow to freeze to death?"

The mention of freezing to death caused us all to look down again at Winant's icy corpse.

"We couldn't go now, at any rate," said Saunders. "Going down the mountain at night would be foolhardy. We could slip into a ravine without ever seeing it."

"Or be attacked by a pack of wolves," Carl added.

"Wolves?" said Benthrop, his voice cracking.

"It's possible. They like to hunt in deep snow because it's harder for their prey to run away from them."

Benthrop took a big gulp of his wine then pulled out a handkerchief and wiped his brow.

"I believe," said Saunders, "that we must take some measures to protect ourselves in case these two deaths were indeed murders. Do you all agree?"

Some of us said yes and some of us just nodded, but no one disagreed. We went into the main room, and Saunders started by asking if anyone knew of any connection between Rich and Winant on the grounds that if we knew what they had in common we might be able to figure out why they were killed and who killed them. No one could think of any common denominator, and so far as anyone knew, Rich and Winant had never met before showing up at the Ranch.

Saunders then guided the conversation to the circumstances surrounding Winant's death. Glover and Wron had placed Rich's body in the freezer shortly after noon, and they took the elk out a few minutes later. It was after eight when Maria discovered Winant's body, so he had to have gone in – or been taken in – sometime within that eight hour span.

"It couldn't have happened while we were cooking," said Betty. "I don't know exactly when that was, but I think we started around two and finished around six thirty, so it had to be before we started cooking or after we started eating when no one was in the kitchen."

"There was a period in there when we were outside gathering juniper berries," Susannah reminded her.

"It could have happened then," Betty agreed.

"It couldn't have been while we were eating," said Teodoro Vasquez, "because that wouldn't have been long enough for him to freeze to death."

"How long does it take?" asked Susannah.

No one seemed to know, but everyone agreed that you could probably survive in a freezer for two or three hours.

"But what if he was already half-frozen when he was put in there?" she asked.

"How would that work?" Glover asked her.

"Someone could have drugged him, dragged him out into the snow to start freezing, then brought him in the back door and stuck him in the freezer while we were eating the elk."

"That seems a little far-fetched," Glover observed.

"I'm still not certain it was a murder," said Vasquez. "I don't like to speak ill of the dead, but Winant seemed sort of strange. Suppose he walked into the freezer, and the door accidentally closed behind him."

"Why would he go into the freezer?"

"Maybe he wanted to say a prayer over Rich's body. Maybe he wanted some ice for a drink, maybe—"

"He didn't drink," I pointed out.

"The door didn't accidentally close," said Maria. She had a blank expression on her face, her eyes unfocused. "I was so shocked when I saw him that I just now realized something. When I went to open the freezer door, I had to remove the padlock."

"The freezer was locked?" Saunders and I said in unison.

"No. The padlock was inserted into the hole, but it wasn't pushed down to lock. I just lifted it up and opened the latch." She turned and looked at us. "Winant might have gone in there voluntarily, but someone else had to hang the padlock in the hole."

Vasquez said, "It could still be an accident. Maybe someone walked by, noticed the padlock wasn't in place, and just hung it in the latch without knowing anyone was inside."

There was a longish silence while we thought about that. I wondered if anyone had accidentally trapped Winant in the freezer and, if so, whether we could expect him or her to admit it. Then another thought occurred to me, and I asked Carl Wron and Glover if they had used the ax on the elk, a question that seemed to be from left field and brought some strange looks my way. They said they had managed with the chain saw and didn't have to resort to the ax. Then I told them I knew when Winant had entered the freezer.

"Shortly after I first heard the chainsaw, I began to hear some muffled thumps. I thought it was the ax sounding muffled because it was coming from outside, but it must have been Winant banging on the inside of the freezer hoping to be released."

"He was in there for eight hours," Susannah said in a pained voice.

"And alive," added Betty.

"Until right after he took his clothes off," said Carla.

A hush fell over the group as everyone pondered how terrifying it must have been to be beating on the thick walls of the freezer as you grew increasingly cold and unable to function, until suddenly your skin began to burn, you stripped off your clothes, then you grew weak and fell and lay there on the floor becoming numb and then passing out.

"I don't think this is getting us anywhere," Saunders said. "I suggest we agree to a set of precautions. First, everyone make sure your doors are locked when you retire for the night. Second, I suggest we have rotating sentries, say on three-hour shifts. It's now almost nine. The first shift could be Vasquez and myself. We will be here in the main room until midnight. At midnight, Glover and Benthrop will relieve us. At three in the morning, Schuze and Wron can take over until six, and at that point we can all get up and there will be no further need for sentries."

"But what if the killer is one of the sentries?" asked Benthrop.

"That's why we have two sentries in each shift."

"Well, that's no good for the person who gets paired with the killer!"

Glover gave Benthrop a wide smile. "Don't worry, professor. If I wanted to kill you, I wouldn't have to wait until we were on sentry duty together."

"Uh, one thing," said Carl. "Some of us may have to be outside our rooms during the night because we don't have private bathrooms." It was a thought that had already arisen in my mind.

"As long as you go directly from your room to the bathroom and back, that should be no problem."

31

"Benthrop's right, Hubie. Someone's killing them off one at a time."

"Who is them?"

"The *Ten Little Indians*."

Susannah was in the bed. I had positioned my pallet on the floor so my feet were against the door. It was locked, of course, but who said the killer couldn't have a key?

"There are only two Indians here, Maria and Srini, and neither one of them has been killed."

"*Ten Little Indians* doesn't refer to the victims, Hubert. It was a mystery novel based on a poem. You've probably heard the poem. 'Ten little Indian boys went out to dine. One choked to death and then there were nine'."

"I think I have heard it, but I don't know the mystery novel."

"It was originally published as *Ten Little N-words*."

"*Ten Little N-words*? That's a strange – oh. The book actually had the N-word in the title?"

"Well, it was back about the time when Lawrence was here, so I guess people still used that word."

"But to put it in the title of a book? That's shocking even for back then."

"I guess someone agreed with you, because they changed it to *Ten Little Indians*."

"I don't know it by that title either. I'm not a fan of murder mysteries, Suze."

"But you are a fan of old movies, so I bet you know *And Then There Were None*."

"I love that film. After the people are stranded on the island, one of the women says, 'The boat won't come until Monday'. Then the character played by C. Aubrey Smith says, in his best stiff-upper-lip fashion, 'No boat will ever come. We're here forever'."

"That's scary, Hubert. You don't think we'll be here forever, do you?"

"I think the Smith character was right – no boat will ever come."

"This is not the time for jokes. What's happening here is exactly what happened in the movie, except the ways they're dying are different. But you'd expect that since this is New Mexico and not England."

"But there are more than ten people here."

"Right. But there are only ten dignitaries. Or were. Now we're down to eight." She furrowed her brow for a moment and then said, "Oh my God! I remember the line for number eight. It goes, 'one overslept and then there were eight'. Remember, Hubie? Winant overslept this morning."

"I'm sure that's just a coincidence, Suze. And he died from freezing, not oversleeping."

I certainly didn't think we were trapped in an English whodunit, and I don't suppose Susannah did either, but it did seem to me there might be an important point in her ramblings. "Saunders said if we knew what the victims had in common, we might be able to figure out why someone might want them dead. Did you pick up any connections between the attendees from talking with them?"

"No. I assumed they were all donors, but we didn't talk about that."

"Did anyone say anything that struck you as surprising or odd?"

She mulled it over for a few seconds. "I was surprised when Srini told me had had been invited at the last minute."

I shrugged. "Probably just the Post Office being slow in delivering his invitation."

"He didn't get it by mail. They phoned him."

"Saunders got his by mail. He just happened to mention it because there was a brochure included with it."

"You think it's a clue?"

"Not that I can see. Maybe Srini was just a last-minute replacement for someone who backed out."

"Maybe someone who was good at predicting the weather," she quipped.

"Did he say why he accepted the invitation?"

"Yes. He thought it would be interesting. But mainly he was afraid he would be violating some American protocol if he refused."

"I wonder why the others agreed to come."

"Maybe they wanted to see the ranch. Or maybe they wanted to hear a lecture about Lawrence or Indian pottery." She passed briefly then asked, "Where's the old pot you brought?"

"I left it on the table next to the projector."

She shook her head. "We moved all the tables over for dinner, and we had to take the laptop and projector off the table you used before we moved it. The pot wasn't there. Are you sure you didn't put it back in the Bronco?"

"Positive. Maybe someone moved it while you were dragging the other tables over for dinner."

She was certain that hadn't happened, but of course anyone could have noticed it sitting there during the day and taken the precaution to move it to a safer place so it wouldn't get accidentally damaged. Maybe Don had put it in the office for safekeeping, I thought. But the thought was also in the back of my mind that someone had stolen it, and I immediately started worrying about that. So I got up and put on trousers and a sweater and went out to the main room where I was greeted by suspicious looks.

32

Vasquez and Saunders were on sentry duty and taking their responsibility seriously.

"Where are you going?" Saunders asked me.

"I just realized I don't know where my Anasazi pot is, and I'm worried about it."

"I'm sorry Schuze, but we can't allow you to roam around looking for your pot. We have to assume that anyone could be the killer."

I had started back to the bedroom when Agatha Cruz came down the hall. She was wearing a frumpy long robe and pink fuzzy slippers. She appeared to have layers of warm clothing under the robe. She resembled a garbage bag stuffed with newspapers.

"Can we help you, Ms. Cruz?" asked Saunders.

"I'm scared of staying alone. Can I stay with Ms. Glain?"

Saunders looked at Vasquez who shrugged, and Saunders told her it would be alright if Ms. Glain agreed.

Agatha was knocking on Glain's door when Susannah came out into the hall. Saunders asked her what she was doing, and she said she got worried when I didn't come back and came out to see if anything was the matter.

Then Patel came out and asked what all the racket was about, and Vasquez and Saunders rose up from their chairs and started trying to get everyone back into their rooms. Canon came out and asked why so many people were roaming around when we were supposed to have sentries. They told him to go back to his room and not become part of the problem, but he asked Robert Saunders why he had not been chosen as one of the sentries, and Robert started explaining to him that there were only six slots, and he just picked people at random, but Canon didn't buy that and kept pressing him about whether there was really another reason he had been left off sentry duty.

Then Carl Wron came out to go to the bathroom but stopped when he saw the crowd and asked why everyone was up, which only added to the confusion because Saunders and Vasquez were trying to answer questions and watch everyone at the same time.

Then Maria came out. She was wearing a tee-shirt that revealed a substantial portion of her legs. They were thick but not fat looking, and they were very nicely shaped, just the sort of legs needed to properly support a pleasingly plump woman. At the bottom of her legs she had the requisite number of feet, each with the standard numbers of toes, and each toe had a nail at its end, nicely trimmed and painted red. It took me a while to establish all this, and I may have missed a few things that were going on in the crowd, but that's just because I'm a man and therefore not very adept at multitasking.

When I had finished visually reconnoitering Maria's legs, I looked up at her and she was staring right into my eyes, and I felt like I had been caught in the act, although I wasn't really doing anything except looking. I felt even warmer in my sweater. But she was smiling at me, so I didn't feel all that bad. In fact, I felt remarkably good.

She stepped over close to me and stood on tippy-toes so that she could whisper in my ear, something that is a rare experience for me. Not having my ear whispered into - that happens to me about as often as it does to most people, I suppose. The unusual part was having someone need to stand on tippy-toes to do the whispering.

"Betty asked me to ask you if you would be willing to switch rooms."

"She wants Susannah and me to move into your room and let you and Betty move into ours?"

She giggled. "No, silly. She wants you and me to trade. I would share a room with Susannah and you would share a room with Betty."

"Oh."

Sometimes I'm a bit slow on the uptake when it comes to 'relationships'.

But after I finally grasped the implications of the question, I realized there were more implications than I had grasped.

My mind was racing. It crossed my mind (on the second or third lap of the race) that maybe Betty hadn't asked that question at all and this was some sort of test. Then it crossed my mind that it would be good to know who had been playing footsy with me at dinner. Then it crossed my mind that maybe Betty was the murderer and she wanted me alone to make me victim number three. Then it crossed my mind that maybe Maria was the murderer and she wanted to be alone with Susannah to make her victim number three.

Then Howard Glover came out and said, "What the hell is going on out here?" and we all fell silent and turned to him.

Just at that moment, Glain opened her door and Agatha Cruz, looking frail and scared, asked Carla if she could stay with her. Carla said yes, and the two of them went into Carla's room and we all heard the bolt slide into place.

"Everyone get back in your rooms," commanded Glover.

I looked at Maria, shrugged, and went back to my room. Saved by the bell. I hoped. I hadn't agreed to share a room with Betty which would have ruined my chances with Maria. And for all I knew, I may have prevented another murder.

To tell the truth, I wasn't anxious to jump into bed with either Betty or Maria. I like sex as much as most people do, and I found them both attractive, but I've always thought it prudent to get to know a woman before going to bed with her. It's not a matter of some grand principle. It's just that having sex with someone creates a sort of bond. I don't mean you have to do the honorable thing and get married. I always thought that was silly. But once you've had sex, the relationship between you changes. That's not bad, necessarily. In fact, usually it's a good change. But it's not one I like to rush into because the woman in question might turn out to be someone you don't want to go to the next stage with. I'm not saying that I've never had sex with a woman I just met, but it's not my customary practice.

Take Stella, for example. Stella and I met in an elevator, and she started flirting with me. I didn't realize she was flirting with me at the time. Susannah explained it to me later after I told her about the conversation. Then I went to visit Stella a day or two later in her apartment, and – well – to put it bluntly, she seduced me. Mind you, I'm not putting the blame on her. I'm an adult and responsible for my own behavior. I could have resisted.

Or maybe not. She was gorgeous, shapely, and so alluring that I just couldn't think of any reason to resist. What was the point I was trying to make here? When I start thinking about Stella, my mind sort of... Oh, now I remember. The point is that I was attracted to both Betty and Maria, but I was glad the circumstances were such that I didn't have a chance to give in to temptation. And although Dolly had said she didn't want to see me again, I was hoping that was just temporary.

33

When we got back to the room, Susannah said she couldn't get Winant off her mind.

"Freezing to death must be horrible, Hubie."

"We don't know that. No one who froze to death has ever come back to tell us if it was horrible."

"We should ask Cyril's great-grandfather. Maybe he knows someone in the spirit world who froze to death."

"I heard something like that. Two men met at the pearly gates and struck up a conversation. The first man said he froze to death. The second man says he had a heart attack. He said he knew his wife was cheating on him so he went home early to try to catch her in the act. He ran into their bedroom where he found her undressed but alone. He ran down to the basement, but no man was hiding there. He ran up to the second floor, but no man was hiding there either. He ran up to the attic, and no one was there. He ran downstairs, through the kitchen, and out into the garage, but still found no one. Then he had a heart attack from all that running up and down stairs and died. 'Too bad you didn't check the freezer on your way through the kitchen,' says the first man. 'If you had, we would both still be alive'."

"That's a terrible joke, Hubert."

"Yeah, but it took your mind off Winant."

"True. And he was a disagreeable guy anyway. You know what I most disliked about him?"

I bit. "What?"

"His frozen countenance."

I laughed.

Neither of us felt like sleeping. I doubt anyone in the building could sleep under the circumstances. So Susannah suggested we try to figure out who the killer was. We all wanted to know who it was so we could stop him. Or her. But Susannah is hooked on murder mysteries and found it exciting to be in the middle of a real one.

For my part, I was feeling responsible for making people believe there had been two murders. Even though I thought I was right, there remained a sliver of doubt. Rich may have fallen into the bath. He may have used both an electric shaver and disposable blades. For all I know, he may have enjoyed icy baths.

Winant may have gone in the freezer to cool off. Maybe he had taken a vow of chastity so that being icy cold was a blessing for him. Maybe someone came along and accidentally trapped him inside by hanging the lock in the latch and was afraid to admit it. That's a lot of maybes. But it could happen.

"I think the best suspect is Vasquez," Susannah volunteered.

"Why?"

"He keeps clinging to the idea that the deaths were accidents. If you want to kill a whole group of people one by one, it's easier if you can convince them the deaths are accidents. That way they aren't on guard against a killer."

"But he's also the one that keeps saying we should call the authorities," I pointed out.

"That's just a ploy to throw suspicion away from himself," she countered. "He knows we can't call the authorities. And on top of that, he's a lobbyist."

"Good point."

"Of course it could be Saunders," she said.

"How do you figure that?"

"Because he's a judge and he sort of took charge after we found the first body. Remember that in the movie, the murderer turns out to be a retired judge, but you don't suspect him because he takes charge of the group and seems to be trying to reveal the killer and stop the killings. It's clever, isn't it, Hubie? You pretend to be hunting the killer, so no one thinks you *are* the killer."

"You told me there are no coincidences, remember? Well, it would be quite a coincidence if what was happening here turned out to mirror what happened in an Agatha Christie mystery."

"It wouldn't be a coincidence if the killer got his ideas from reading mysteries. It could happen, Hubie. You know what they say – 'Life imitates art'."

I snapped my fingers. "We need pictures."

"I didn't see any security cameras."

"I don't mean pictures of the killer in the act. I mean pictures of everyone here."

"Of course!" she said, and then hesitated. "Why do we need pictures?"

"Because someone here isn't who he says he is."

"I knew it! Who is it?"

"If I knew that, we wouldn't need the pictures. Did you bring a camera?"

"No, but you did."

I frowned at her.

"The cell phone Tristan gave you is also a camera," she said.

"But we're out of range for cell phones."

"Jeez. Give me the thing. You don't have to be in range for the camera to work."

I looked out the window and saw falling particles. I couldn't tell whether it was sleet, snow, or rain. I opened the window but couldn't feel anything because of the deep eaves. I had to lean out the window and extend my arm full length to discover it was a warm gentle rain. That's a New Mexico spring for you – a blizzard one day, a tropical drizzle the next.

Of course the rain was welcome. It would begin to melt the snow. We could all go home, and there would be no more murders. Maybe the police could eventually find out who did it. I hoped justice would be served. But frankly, it was not my problem. Unlike the other murders I had accidentally gotten involved in, I wouldn't have to figure out who the killer was.

34

Carl Wron and I spent an uneventful shift as sentries. Shortly after six, the guests started to straggle out of their rooms. By seven most people were up and in the main room. Glain and Cruz hadn't come out, but the ones who did must not have gotten much sleep. They looked like zombies.

The snow cover had been reduced from several feet to several inches by the rain. We could have driven away, but we agreed we should stay put until the police came. Benthrop said he wasn't staying a minute more, but after Glover threatened to stop him by force if necessary, he took a chair and sulked.

It was decided Canon would drive to Taos and bring back the police since he was in charge of the facility where it had all happened. He got in a pickup with a university seal on the door, and we watched him drive away with relief. It seemed like our nightmarish weekend was nearing an end.

Maria made coffee, and we all remained in the main room on the grounds that there is safety in numbers. We sat around sipping coffee until someone suggested we should wake Glain and Cruz, so Betty went and knocked on the door.

There was no answer. She knocked louder. Still no answer. We all looked at each other, and what we saw looking back at us were faces full of angst. Even though no one said a word, we arose almost as one and dragged ourselves into the hall where Betty was standing at the door to Glain's room. Howard Glover stepped up to the door and slammed an open palm against it, creating a detonation that was probably audible inside the freezer and loud enough to wake both Fred Rich and Charles Winant.

Still no answer. Someone asked if anyone had a key. Saunders said Don probably did, but he was gone, and Betty observed that a key wouldn't do us any good anyway since we'd all heard the bolt slide into place last night. Howard looked around at us, and we all nodded a silent permission. He took one step back, lowered his shoulder and rammed it into the door. It was a cheap hollow-core number and he was a big solid-core man. The door split open like a dried gourd.

Carla Glain was on the floor, a pool of black blood around her head. Betty screamed, Susannah gasped, and Patel let out a small shriek. Glover bent down to take another look and confirmed what we all knew.

Like a squad of shell-shocked soldiers, we stood there staring at her until Patel spotted a piece of paper on the bed. He picked it up and handed it to Glover who read it and handed it to Saunders who held it up for us all to see. Words and letters had been cut out of magazines and taped to the paper. They spelled out a message: "They were evil. I killed them. Now I can rest in peace. Agatha."

After we looked at the paper, we all looked at the window. It was open. We walked around the bed to get a better look and there on the floor were Agatha Cruz's blue robe and pink fuzzy slippers, the floor around them soaked with rain from the open window.

"She killed Glain during the night and escaped out the window," said Vasquez in a tone more of resignation than concern.

"I don't think so," replied Glover. "Glain's head was bashed in. I don't think that old lady would have the strength to do that."

"Yeah," said Susannah, "and I can't see her climbing out a window either. On top of that, why would she write her confession that way? If she's going to admit to the murders, what's the point of disguising her handwriting? The real killer must be trying to frame her."

"Then where is she?" asked Saunders.

"The real killer must have taken her," said Susannah. "He brained Glain, gagged and bound Cruz and took her out the window."

"Why did he take her robe and slippers off?" Saunders retorted.

"So she couldn't run away. Maybe he wanted a hostage."

"But we had sentries all night. It couldn't have been one of the sentries because the other one on duty would have seen him leave. And no one left a bedroom other than the sentries after Cruz went into Glain's room."

"That's it!" shouted Susannah. "We've all been assuming the murderer had to be one of us. But it must be someone who's been sneaking in."

"I don't think so," I said. "No one came into Fred Rich's room through a window. The snow was piled up against the panes when we found him. There are only two doors to the outside of this building, and with all of us milling around, I don't see how someone could walk in out of the snow and not be noticed. Even if no one saw him, we would have heard the door or at least seen the snow on the floor. On top of that, where would a killer hide in a blizzard for two days?"

"We can't be absolutely certain no one came in," she said dejectedly, and I felt bad about deflating her theory. Then she perked up and said, "Where would Cruz get a dull instrument?"

I told everyone that Cruz looked like she had things under her clothes that night when I saw her in the hall, and for all I knew, one of those things could have been a hammer or an iron bar.

"It had to be Canon," said Benthrop, his eyes wide with excitement. "He came in here through the window after he left for town and killed Glain and snatched Cruz."

Saunders gave him a withering look. "We all saw Canon drive off in the truck."

"He could have come back."

"Without us hearing the truck?"

"Maybe he walked back," insisted Benthrop.

"Wouldn't matter," chimed in Glover. "She's been dead for several hours. If Canon did it, he had to do it long before he left for Taos."

Glover said we should try to track Cruz, so we all traipsed outside as if we knew what we were doing. There were still a few inches of snow, so we could see the tracks. Footsteps led from below Glain's window out to the cliff Canon had warned us about.

We crept up to the edge. I did less creeping than the others. I have severe acrophobia. We peered down at thick brush two-hundred feet below. If anyone had jumped, fallen, or been thrown over the cliff, we couldn't tell. We circled around the building and found no other tracks except those leading out from the front door to where Canon had entered the truck. We were standing by where the truck had been parked when Vasquez noted belatedly that we shouldn't be disturbing a crime scene, so we all went back inside.

Betty said, "That crazy old hag killed them and then jumped off the cliff."

"Why did she take her nightgown and slippers off first?" asked Susannah.

Betty shrugged. "Maybe she wanted to make sure she would freeze to death just in case she survived the fall."

"Maybe it was another case of paradoxical undressing," said Susannah jokingly.

That brought a few stern looks her way.

"It seems to me," I ventured, "that she didn't jump. She wanted to make us think she jumped. That's why she worded the confession like a suicide note. I already mentioned her robe looked bulky. She could have had regular clothes on underneath which she wore to make her escape."

"So where is she?" asked Glover. "There were no tracks except to the cliff."

There were a couple of minutes of silence while we all thought about it. I was the first to speak. "Maybe she had ropes under her robe and rappelled down the cliff."

Glover was incredulous. "That old lady?"

"Her robe must really have been stuffed, Hubie," said Susannah. "You've given her a weapon, a second set of clothes, and ropes under there. Why not a parachute?"

I turned up my palms but said nothing.

"I don't think Cruz could rappel down the cliff, but a good climber could come up that way," said Glover, "so maybe someone did come in through the window, kill Glain and take Cruz away. That would explain why the only tracks were between the window and the cliff."

"I knew it was someone from outside," said Susannah.

I didn't believe that but had no better theory to offer. I went over and sat down next to Susannah and asked her in a whisper if she had all the pictures. She said she had them all except for Rich and Winant. She had surreptitiously snapped one of Glain on the floor. I whispered to her to go to the freezer and get pictures of Rich and Winant, and she made a face like she was licking a lemon.

Adele the Serving Wench was heading down the hall and Benthrop demanded to know where she was going. She said she was going to the bathroom, and Benthrop insisted that one of the other women go with her in case she was the murderer.

"Why would one of us want to go to the bathroom with the murderer?" Betty asked quite sensibly.

"Well," squeaked Benthrop, "we can't let her go alone."

"Why?" asked Glover. "You afraid she might kill herself?"

Maria suggested wryly that Benthrop should guard the ladies room, but Adele gave her a mean look and continued on down the hall. She returned a few minutes later and everyone watched her silently take a seat at an unoccupied table.

Susannah then announced that she too was going to the bathroom, did not need a chaperone, and would return shortly. I noticed she had the cell phone in her hand and went down the hall that had the side entrance to the kitchen. She's a trouper.

I took the opportunity to ask the group if anyone had moved the pot I used during my talk, but they all denied knowing what had happened to it.

The camaraderie I had sensed during the elk dinner was gone, or perhaps it had existed only in my imagination. We sat in sullen silence until the police arrived.

I passed the time thinking about my missing pot. Or, more accurately, how I felt about it. I felt angry and cheated. I felt – and I generally don't like the way this word is thrown around these days – violated.

And guilty. Because if I didn't like the way having my pot stolen made me feel, then how could I justify stealing pots myself?

The answer is that the previous owners of the pots I dig up are dead and therefore can't feel the way I felt. I would never steal a pot from another living potter, Native American or otherwise. But was I just rationalizing? I thought about it long and hard and decided quite honestly that I wasn't.

Of course the Duran pot didn't belong to some prehistoric potter. But who did it belong to? Cyril believed it still belonged to his great-grandfather. But maybe the university had some legal claim based on something like adverse possession. After all, it had been in their possession for eighty years. But judging from the fact that it was sitting under a desk in an unlocked cabin, they probably didn't even know they had it. It deserved better. At least I knew the pueblo would be a good home for it, and it would be among people who would honor it.

Rationalization? Maybe, but I felt returning the pot to Cyril was the right thing to do. I put that belief to the ultimate test by asking myself what I would do if he failed to give me the three Dulcinea pots in return. It made me feel good to realize that I would give him the pot anyway.

Of course I was hoping it wouldn't turn out that way.

The next few hours are muddled in my memory. All I remember is that the state police arrived, questioned us and let us go home.

35

Tuesday was a good day. I slept until noon then ate a long and leisurely breakfast with a chilled flute of Gruet.

I didn't open the shop until almost two, sold a replica of a San Ildefonso collar pot for a thousand dollars, and was thinking about closing early to celebrate with a nap.

Then Whit Fletcher arrived.

"You don't look happy to see me, Hubert. You got a guilty conscience?"

"Why should I?"

"Maybe stealing all those pots over the years is catching up with you."

"I don't steal them, Whit. They don't belong to anybody."

"That's what you always say." He sidled over to the counter and braced himself against it on one elbow. "Maybe you're worried about those three dead people they found with you up in Taos."

I assumed it had been a big news item, so of course he would know about it. For my part, I was trying to ignore it. I'd spent most of the time since then taking long hot showers, sleeping, eating comfort foods, and reading a book called *Zero*. It's subtitled *The Biography of a Dangerous Idea*. I'm not making this up. It's easy to forget about murder when you're absorbed in such an abstract topic. So maybe I'm weird, but I'm confident it's a better way to pass the time than watching a bunch of idiots pretending to be stranded on a desert island when you know full well there is an entire Hollywood film crew there with air-conditioned trailers and make-up mirrors. Reality television is an oxymoron. And the people in it are genuine morons.

I hadn't read a newspaper or left the building. I don't have many skills, but one of them is the ability to shut things out of my mind. Some people would say that's a handicap rather than a skill, but I've never worried about things just because most other people do. I know I'm supposed to care who gets elected president and who wins on American Idol, but I don't. The two can switch places for all I care. In fact, I suspect we would be better off if they did. So I hadn't spent much time worrying about what had happened at the Ranch. I won't say the images and questions weren't still popping into my mind, but I sent them packing when they did.

I told Fletcher I regretted that three people had been killed, but there was nothing to be gained by me worrying about it.

He shifted his weight to the other elbow and pushed his lank silver hair out of his eyes. "I guess you're right. Still, you've been pretty good at figuring out things like that when you put your mind to it."

"I had a reason to put my mind to it in those cases, Whit. You were accusing me of murder."

"Aw, Hubert, I never done that. I told you I knew you wasn't guilty."

"Well this time I'm not even accused, and I like it that way."

"Sure you do. Anyone would. Nobody wants to be the suspect. But this is a tough case, Hubert. Three people dead, the public's going to expect some action."

He was looking around at the merchandise, something he never does. "Why are you telling me this, Whit? Taos isn't in your jurisdiction."

"That's true, Hubert, but we cops have to work together. It's that whatchamacallit – professional courtesy. I bet even pot thieves do the same sort of thing, help each other out when they can."

His eyes stopped scanning the room and came to rest on the counter in front of me. I said nothing and finally he looked up and made eye contact.

"Whit," I said, "spit it out."

"O.K., you and me been friends a long time, Hubert. I know I had to arrest you a few times, but that was just me doin' my job, no hard feelings either way. And you know I never tried to make it stick 'cause I know you're not the criminal sort 'cept for digging up old pots, and who the hell cares about that? So it would be a feather in my cap if I could solve this here major triple homicide, and I'm asking you to help."

"Why me?"

"You was there, Hubert. You must have noticed things. Like I said, you're pretty good at figuring things out when you put your mind to it. Besides, there's talk of a reward, and we could split it."

I figured as much. Whit has a nose for money. I told him I might want something from him in return. I wanted to recover my Anasazi pot, and I figured I might need police assistance to do so. I couldn't very well file a theft report since I didn't have the legal right to own the pot in the first place. But informal police assistance might be exactly what I would need, so – not for the first time – we agreed to scratch each other's backs.

36

I was in such a good mood on my way to *Dos Hermanas* that I not only cut through the plaza, I even walked up and through the gazebo. In celebration of the fact that I can choose to close any time I want, I was singing

> The man who only lives for making money
> Lives a life that isn't necessarily sunny
> Fall in love and you won't regret it
> Nice work if you can get it
> And you can get it if you try

I fancied that I sounded like Fred Astaire in *A Damsel in Distress.* He was a lot taller and danced better, but I can sing as well as he did.

I told Susannah and Martin about Whit's visit. We hadn't seen Martin since our return from Taos, so she filled him in on our adventure on the mountain.

"You left out the part about how I felt when I found Fidelio Duran's pot."

"It's not Fidelio Duran's pot," she replied. "Dead people don't own things."

"I've been telling you that for years, Suze. That's why it's O.K. to dig up old pots. They belong to the living."

She turned to Martin. "That pot gave Hubie an epiphany."

"And I didn't even smoke it."

She and Martin groaned in unison, and he asked what kind of epiphany.

"I can't describe it."

"I can," said Susannah, "It's called greed."

"Actually, it was quite the opposite. I admit I think of the money when I dig up a pot, but my first thoughts are always about the potter, the sense of connection across time. Maybe this was just a stronger version of that because I knew a few details about the actual potter."

Susannah said to Martin, "He smelled the pot to see if he could detect the stew that was in it eighty years ago."

"The man has a good nose," Martin conceded.

"I couldn't smell anything, of course. And I couldn't really feel anything either. Too cold. But I imagined the warmth of his hands on the pot and the scent of the *chiles* in the stew."

"Oh, brother," said Susannah.

"I know what your epiphany was," Martin announced.

"Was it that I did a good thing taking the pot so it could go home?"

"I don't think it was something you did. Something you realized."

We sat in silence while I tried to figure out what I had realized. "I realized the pot was intimately connected to Fidelio Duran and not to D. H. Lawrence?"

"What else?" he prompted.

"That I didn't own the pot?"

He nodded. "The reason you don't understand the epiphany is you think the feeling of not owning the pot was peculiar to this one incident. Because of the deal you struck with the great-grandson."

"You saying I don't own any of the pots I dig up?"

He shrugged. "Marx said the first form of ownership is tribal."

Susannah turned up her palms. "We're not going to talk about Karl Marx, are we? This is a bar, guys. We should talk about booze, romance, sports or movies."

"Just for a minute," said Martin. "Fidelio Duran wouldn't have thought of the pot as his property. Not because someone else owned it, but because the question wouldn't have occurred to him. He needed a pot, so he made one. Each family made their own pots. Issues of ownership don't arise until a society organizes around the division of labor and people are separated from what they make. When you make a pot in a factory, it doesn't belong to you because it's made to be sold. When you make one in a teepee, it doesn't belong to you because it's *not* made to be sold."

"Yeah, I took Marxism 101," said Susannah. "Workers in complex societies are alienated from the things they create. And I can't believe you said 'teepee'."

"I like the sound of it," he replied.

I still hadn't figured out what Martin was trying to say. "So why don't I own the pots I dig up?"

"Because they were not made to be owned."

"They weren't made to be left in the ground, either."

"You can't own them," he said, "but you can care for them. You realized in Taos that you were just the custodian for that pot. What you didn't realize, but felt in an inchoate way, was that you are *always* just the custodian."

Susannah frowned. "First Marx and now 'inchoate', whatever the hell that means."

"I can see I sometimes have a custodial duty to return pots to someone, like the stolen Ma pots I recovered or the Duran pot. But what about the ones where there is no one to return them to?"

He smiled. "Then your job is to find them a good home."

"And it's O.K. to be paid for that service?"

He held up an empty Tecate can. "You buying?"

I nodded.

37

The first European to see what is now Albuquerque was a captain Alvarado with Conquistador Francisco Vasquez de Coronado's expedition in the 1540s. The settlement along the banks of the Rio Grande wasn't named Albuquerque until many years later when Governor Cuervo y Valdez named the city in honor of the Viceroy of New Spain, the Duke of Alburquerque. The first "r" was dropped at some point. The contemporary New Mexican novelist Rudolfo Anaya claims the dropped "r" was a deliberate attempt to deemphasize the Hispanic roots of my home town. If so, it failed miserably. No matter how you spell Albuquerque, it will always have its Hispanic character.

Like most major cities, Albuquerque sits at a junction, the Rio Grande running north/south and a road running east/west that eventually became Route 66, the Federal Highway from Chicago to Los Angeles. Interstate 40 has supplanted 66 and the old 66 is now known as Central Avenue. The Nob Hill stretch of Central has been undergoing an uneven gentrification. The area further east is home mostly to low-rent businesses – small cafes, specialty shops, a few rundown motels, and the odd adult bookstore and baseball trading card establishment. One old edifice a handful of yards from the intersection with San Mateo is called the Alvarado building, and it looks like it might have been established by the captain of that name in Coronado's expedition. At the back of that building and next to a nail salon run by Vietnamese immigrants, I found the office of the Albuquerque Chapter of Justice Now.

I opened the glass door and stepped into a room with faded orange shag carpet, paneled walls of fake oak, an acoustic ceiling and a buzzing fluorescent light with one tube blinking at random. There was a dodgy-looking couch with stained cushions, a glass coffee table covered with pamphlets, and a metal desk of the sort usually found at used furniture shops. A nameplate on the desk identified it as the station of Wanda Reynolds, but Wanda was away from her desk.

I heard murmurs in an adjoining room and cleared my throat. A gawky woman with large blue eyes and straggly blond hair came in from the next room and asked if she could help me. She had a friendly innocent look and a nice smile.

I told her I was Hubert Schuze and had come about Carla Glain. She burst into tears and hugged me. She smelled like baby powder.

She stepped back and grasped both my hands. "We are so glad you have come. Please come in and meet the staff." Before I could react, she dragged me into the next room. There were some candles burning on a folding table in front of a glossy picture of Carla Glain that looked like a blow-up from a high school album.

"I want you to meet our team leader, Fred Givens. And this is Rhonda Marisol. She's a field agent like Carla was. This is Tommy Behrent, he's our fiscal officer. He's supposed to be part-time, but like everyone else, he's so dedicated that he works from dawn to dusk. This is our client services coordinator, Sylvia True, and this is Ron Gore, the other field agent. And of course I'm Wanda, the administrative assistant."

I decided against constructing a mental walk. I had no reason to remember these people.

"Wanda is the real boss," said Givens. Everyone tittered appreciatively. "Now that you're here, we can get started."

I was as confused as a rabbi at a rodeo. "I don't really know what—"

"Of course," Givens cut in. "How unthinking of me. I guess we're all still so upset that we're not thinking very clearly. Let me tell you what we have planned. We want you to go first and just say whatever you want to about Carla. Then each of us who worked with her will say whatever comes into our hearts. Then we'll have a moment of silence. Carla was not one to stand on ceremony, and she didn't care for fancy things, so we just all decided something low-key would be the sort of memorial service she would have wanted."

They all smiled and looked at me. I had no idea why they thought I was there for the memorial service. Mistaken identity – that must be it. I started to tell them they must have me confused with someone else when Fred Givens smiled at me and said, "Whenever you're ready, Mr. Schuze."

38

"That's awful, Hubie. What did you do?"

"I gave a eulogy. What else could I do?"

It was a warm evening on the veranda at *Dos Hermanas*.

"But you hardly knew her. What did you say?"

What I had said was that we were gathered not to mourn because mourning cannot be done in the space of a mere afternoon and would be something we would each do in our own way and in our own time. We were gathered instead to celebrate the life of Carla Glain. And I said it was a life worthy of celebration because it was a life dedicated to the betterment of others. I said the best testimony to the effectiveness of her efforts was the esteem in which her colleagues held her. That even though I did not know them well (I did not mention that I knew them about as well as I knew Glain), I could see that esteem in their faces. I said their remarks would be more meaningful than mine, and with that in mind, I would keep my own words brief. I noted that she was dedicated to justice, fiercely protective of society's most vulnerable members, and not easily swayed by social norms."

"That last phrase was a zinger, Hubie. Not only was she not swayed by social norms, she threw them in your face."

"They saw it as positive."

"Of course they did. With all that first stuff, you made her sound like mother Theresa."

"It was a eulogy, Suze. I couldn't very well say she had the personality of a barracuda. But you'll love my last line: She faced the evils of destiny and deflected them with good."

"You made that up?"

"No, I remembered it from that book I read on Pythagoras. It's from one of his poems."

"And they bought it?"

"They loved it. There wasn't a dry eye in the crowd. Afterwards, they heaped praises on me. I'm telling you, Suze, it was all I could do to get out of there. I may have a new career as a eulogist."

"Eulogist is not an occupation, Hubert. What I don't get is how they knew who you were and why they expected you."

"Turns out all our names were listed in the article in the paper about the deaths at the Ranch. Fred Givens has a friend at the paper, and he asked his friend to try and contact one of us to see if we would attend the memorial. They wanted someone who had 'been with her at the end' as they put it. They seemed to be under the impression that we were a group, that we knew each other or had some common interest."

"We did have a common interest," said Susannah, "getting out alive. I'm not surprised the friend at the newspaper couldn't talk anyone into going. And I can understand that when you showed up, they assumed he had sent you. But why did you go there?"

"I already told you. I agreed to help Fletcher solve the murders. I figured the best way to start was to interview everyone who was at the Ranch."

"What was it, Hubert, a memorial service or a séance? 'Cause unless it was a séance, I don't see how you could interview Carla Glain."

"I'll interview the survivors, but I also want to find out everything I can about the victims."

"So what did you learn about Carla?"

"Almost nothing. She didn't attend college and had no money, so she was almost certainly not a donor to UNM. However, they told me she worked as a volunteer in the Governor's campaign, so maybe the

University invited her because they thought she had some political clout."

"Being a volunteer doesn't give you clout. There are hundreds of them. I'll bet the Governor wouldn't even recognize most of them."

"I don't know if he would have recognized her, but he did appoint her to the Gaming Commission."

"What? She's an expert on Monopoly or Chinese checkers?"

"The Gaming Commission regulates gambling, Suze."

"Gambling is not a game."

"I guess Carla agreed with you. I asked why she would want to be on the Gaming Commission, and Givens said she wanted to advocate for the poor who lose their meager paychecks at the tables every week."

"So now what?"

"I'm going to see someone else from the group. Did you make prints of those pictures?"

She had shown me the pictures on the little screen of the cell phone, but I had asked her to make what are called "hard copies" even though they are on paper which is not hard. The excuse I gave was that the pictures on the screen were too small, but the truth is I was afraid I might push the wrong button and erase them.

She took the pictures out of her satchel, and we looked at them together. Carla Glain looked worse in death than she had in life. I suppose that's true of most people, but the dried blood on the floor next to her made it even worse.

Winant and Rich looked very cold. All the other pictures were decent enough likenesses to serve my purpose.

I removed Srinivasa Patel's picture from the stack and handed it to her.

"You can start with this one," I said.

Her face brightened and her big brown eyes shone. "Really, Hubie? You want me to help?"

"Have I ever figured anything out without you?"

"Wow. This is so exciting. What do you want me to ask him?"

"I have no idea because I don't have any theory about what happened. Just ask anything you think might be useful."

She hesitated for a moment and then said, "You don't think it's Srini, do you?"

"I don't, but be careful anyway."

"Who are you taking?"

I reached into the pile of pictures at random and pulled out Carl Wron.

39

Carl Wron's ranch was just a few miles south of the intersection of U.S. Highway 64 and State Highway 505. 505 used to be the area code for the entire state of New Mexico. Now we have two area codes. I don't know whether that reflects more people or just more phones. Everyone seems to have two these days.

The trip took me back through Taos, but instead of going north towards the Lawrence Ranch, I headed east on U.S. 64. There was almost no traffic once I got away from Taos, and I enjoyed the view of Wheeler Peak to the north. At over thirteen thousand feet, it's capped by snow most of the year, and on this crisp clear day, the view was spectacular. From there, the highway passes through Eagle Nest and Cimarron.

I arrived around four and drove down a gravel road to a small wooden house with a painted metal roof. A large elm showed from behind the house and a couple of mulberry trees grew on either side of the front porch. Except for those three trees, the landscape was all high grassland. A herd of buffalo grazed in the distance.

Wron emerged from the house as I approached. He was wearing worn jeans, a white western shirt with mother-of-pearl buttons, beat-up old boots with riding heels. He took off a straw before shaking my hand

and bidding me welcome. His skin was white above the line the hat made on his head. Below the line he was leathery and brown.

We sat on the front porch and drank lemonade. He told me he used to ranch the area but sold the land after his wife had died of cancer. His only child, a son named Pete, died in Viet Nam.

"The new owners are in the big house," he told me, saying it like I was familiar with the layout. "This was the hired man's house, but they let me stay here as part of the deal. I'm happy they took the big place. They're keeping it up real well."

He stared off into the distance. "Yes sir," he said absently, "real well."

I waited for him to say something else, but he didn't, so I asked him why he had gone to the event at Taos.

He chuckled. "Truth is, I was interested in seeing the spread up there. It's awful high for ranching. Course with that blizzard, I didn't really get the opportunity."

He looked at me and then said, "But of course what you want to know is why they invited me." He handed me the letter of invitation he had received. It was personalized and on good embossed stationery from the UNM Development Office.

"Pete went to the University," he continued. "He seemed to like it real well. His mother was right proud of him. He got good marks." He fell silent for a minute before speaking again. "When I sold the place, I didn't have need for the money, so I gave it to the University. Now they invite me to everything, football games, symphonies, you name it."

"You ever go?"

"Too far," he said. Then he smiled to himself. "Truth is, I don't like the city. Pete liked it, though. Sure did."

"Did you know any of the other people at the Ranch?"

"No. I've seen Glover on television a few times. He seems like a nice fella. Miss Shanile was nice too. I could take a shine to her if I was younger. I'm not much for socializing, but they all seemed like good folks." He turned to me. "You think one of them killed those three?"

"It looks that way."

He shook his head and stared off again into the distance. In the house, the phone rang, but he made no move to answer it. After about a dozen rings, it stopped.

"Let me show you around," he said, and we got into his pick-up and drove out across the grass toward the buffalo. He showed me a small stream that cut through his land and fed into the Canadian River and several places where he had rigged up diversions to create watering holes for the cattle. He took me to an outcrop of rocks with petroglyphs and asked me if I knew what they symbolized. I did and was happy to explain them to him. He drove me by the big house and the barns. The tour ended at a little chapel next to which were the graves of his father, mother, sister, wife and son. We stood there for several minutes. A faint breeze fanned the tall grass and a lump formed in my throat.

Carl offered to buy me dinner. Even though it was four hours back to Albuquerque and I hate to drive after dark, I couldn't say no. We went to the Colfax Tavern. I wanted to try their green chile cheeseburger, but Carl said it was spaghetti night, and for three fifty a plate, you couldn't complain about the quantity, the quality, or the price. Several ranchers stopped by his table to say hello and he introduced them to me like I was a celebrity.

It was almost dark by the time I started back, so I drove further east until I hit Interstate 25 a little south of Raton and flew back to Albuquerque on the freeway. On the way, I thought about what I had learned. Wron was a donor and he manifestly was not the killer. Neither piece of information seemed worth the trip. Spending the time with him did.

40

I slept late the next morning and had a leisurely breakfast after which I pushed the plate back and put the "hard copy" photos in front of me on the table. I reached in at random and drew out Teodoro Vasquez.

I put his picture aside and reached in again and pulled out Adele the Serving Wench. I put that picture aside. After two or three more random draws, Betty Shanile's picture came up, so I decided she would be the next person I'd interview.

I could have kept drawing until I got Maria, but she lived in Taos, and I wasn't up to a third trip there in the same month.

Betty agreed to meet me for lunch, but I sensed a lack of enthusiasm in her voice. The look on her face reinforced that sense when I sat down across from her at a place that has since closed. The restaurant business is tough under the best of circumstances, but a restaurant in Albuquerque that serves French food is a risky investment. It probably didn't help that the place was in a strip mall.

I now wonder if the negative energy of our lunch contributed to their demise. Except for *Dos Hermanas Tortilleria*, I have a spotty history with restaurants. I was involved with another European one called *Schnitzel* that also went belly up, but that's another story.

Except for the look on Betty's face, the inside of the restaurant was inviting, especially since our table did not look out on the midday traffic on Wyoming Boulevard.

She had an empty glass in her hand. A waiter asked me what I wanted to drink and Betty told him she wanted another vodka rocks before I had a chance to answer.

So it was going to be that kind of lunch.

I told the waiter to have the bartender surprise me. He brought Betty her second vodka rocks (at least it was the second so far as I knew) and me a small chilled glass of St. Jean dry vermouth. I thought to myself, that's what happens when you do something rash like asking the bartender to surprise you.

The waiter also brought both of us an *amuse bouche* consisting of a piece of flatbread with house-made fish paste topped by a strip of roasted green chile. It was spectacular, and the vermouth was a perfect pairing. I decided I liked the place.

Betty signaled the waiter for another drink and said to me, "Why are you here, Hubie?"

Susannah had asked me the same question in our room at the Ranch that first night, but this time there was no doubt about the question's meaning. I decided to play dumb anyway, and I replied by asking her if that was a philosophical question.

She gave me a sarcastic smile and finished her second vodka just as the third one arrived.

"I guess it's obvious why you're here," I said. "You like the bartender."

Another insincere smile. I buried my face in the menu while deciding whether to order, try to find out why she was so grumpy, or just leave. The only green chile was on the *amuse bouche*, and I wondered whether they would let me order an entire plate of them. There was nothing else on the menu I wanted. In fact, there were few things on the menu I could pronounce.

"You didn't answer my question, Hubie."

I looked up at her and smiled. "I'm here to have lunch with you. I wanted to see you again."

"Did you and Susannah break up?"

"We're just friends, Betty."

"Is Maria Salazar also your friend?" she asked, putting a leering stress on the word 'friend'."

"I thought she was *your* friend," I said. "You were the one rooming with her."

A small fissure appeared in her stony countenance. "That's a clever comeback." She took another gulp of vodka. "Am I being difficult?"

That's another one of those questions that raises a man's antennae, the sort of question that comes with a little invisible warning label that says, "Answer at your own risk."

"Perhaps enigmatic," I said and tried to give her my best boyish smile.

"A woman of mystery?"

"An attractive woman of mystery," I added.

A smile. Small but sincere. "Flattery will get you anywhere."

I wasn't sure where I wanted flattery to get me, so I suggested we order. She selected *Coq au vin*, and I followed her lead because I know very little about French cuisine and the situation was difficult enough without ordering some dish that might turn out to be raw chopped steak with capers.

She seemed less unhappy with me and less on edge, but I didn't know whether it was the small talk or the vodka that was putting her at ease. I was relieved when the food came and gave us something to talk about other than my putative relationships with Susannah and Maria.

I never knew the simple act of braising chicken in wine could produce such a delicious result. Betty explained that it wasn't just chicken. The dish has to be made with a rooster, preferable an old one because the connective tissue is the source of the flavor.

"I'm surprised the meat isn't tough since it came from an old rooster," I remarked.

She smiled and said, "Give an old cock enough wine and it becomes soft."

I was just sipping some vermouth, and I almost spewed it out. Obviously, she was not through making me uncomfortable.

She ordered vodka number... well, I lost count, and we managed a pleasant conversation despite two or three more zingers from her.

She paid the bill because she knew the staff and my attempts to intervene were rebuffed. I insisted on driving her home because she was in no condition to get behind the wheel. She asked if that was just a ploy to get in her house, and I said it was in a tone I hoped was somewhere between serious and joking.

I had to steady her as we walked up to an impressive house in the Four Hills area, what I think they call 'mid-century' architecture built of long skinny bricks with a flat roof and wide rectangular windows. The lush Bermuda-grass lawn sloped graciously to the road and the brick pathway to the door wound between old western catalpas that had grown into interesting shapes. The house looked comfortable and impressive, an unusual combination, and I wanted to see the inside, but it was not to be.

By the time we reached the door, she had her key in her hand. She turned and gave me a rather longish kiss, and I have to admit I liked the way her ample lips felt against mine. Then she unlocked her door and went inside without saying a word.

41

I hadn't opened the shop that morning because I was tired from the round trip to see Carl Wron, and I didn't open it that afternoon because I had consumed two glasses of vermouth during lunch and needed a nap. I occasionally have Gruet with breakfast and almost always have a drink or two or three in the evening without any ill effects, but even moderate drinking in the middle of the day knocks me out. It must have something to do with metabolism.

I felt great when I awoke and even better after I took a long hot shower, so I was in a good mood when I walked over to *Dos Hermanas*.

After I told Susannah about the lunch with Betty, she said, rather unsympathetically, "So you just let her go into the house and shut the door?"

"What was I supposed to do, break in?"

"Jeez, Hubie. The woman was pleading for some reassurance, and all you did was parry her double *entendres*."

"She wasn't pleading for anything. She was asking me if you and I had broken up after I had clearly explained to her in Taos that we're just friends."

"When did you do that?"

"Do what?"

"Explain to her that we're just friends."

"Um, I think it was before my presentation the next morning after the initial confusion the first night."

She just shook her head.

"It wasn't then?"

"No Hubert. She came out at the last minute, remember? She almost missed the start of your lecture."

"Oh, right. It must have been after the lecture."

"Would that be before or after we found Fred Rich's body?"

"Oh, right. You know, it was definitely before the presentation because I was drinking coffee and...oops, it was Maria I explained it to. Maria told me that morning that Betty had told her that I might come to their room, and if I did then Maria should leave and room with you. But I didn't go to the room, and Betty told Maria it was because I was sleeping with you."

"That's just great. No one asks me if I'm willing to room with Maria, and Betty still thinks I'm some pushover you picked up on your way to the Ranch."

"But Maria knows we're just friends, and she was rooming with Betty, so surely she must have explained it to her."

She stared at me, slowly shaking her head. "Hubie, you are so dense."

"Well, I don't deny that I get lost in the hedges occasionally, but what is it this time?"

"Maria is hot for you, Hubie. And she has a competitive advantage over Betty. She's knows you're available. Betty doesn't."

"Are you saying Maria wouldn't tell Betty you and I are friends? That sounds disingenuous."

"*C'est amour.*"

I was confused. I had been fairly certain that Maria had flirted with me, but I didn't realize it was so obvious that Susannah would have noticed. And Maria seemed like a nice person, and now I'm told she misled Betty. Or did she?

"I guess you're right," I said. "They probably realized via some mysterious woman-thing communication that they both liked me, and it would be awkward to talk about it, so they just discussed cooking and traded their favorite recipes."

"Oink."

I ignored that and said, "But that couldn't be right, because on the second night, Maria told me Betty wanted to switch rooms, which I first misunderstood as a request for you and I to take Betty and Maria's room so that they could have ours. But what the proposal actually intended was putting me with Betty and you with Maria. Of course I realized even then that the proposal may not have come from Betty at all and might have been a test or a trick, and I was grateful I didn't have to answer because Howard Glover ordered us all back to our rooms and sentries were guarding the hall, and a lot of good that did Carla Glain."

Susannah looked confused.

"O.K.," I continued, "forget Carla Glain. There's nothing I can do for her, and at least I gave her a nice eulogy."

But the business with Betty and Maria was still confusing me, and I realized how accurate Susannah was in calling me dense. But I'm not alone, am I? Do men really understand romance? Sometimes I wish romance were like math with nice precise answers. But it's like statistics or, even worse, probability, because you never know the true odds, you don't know how much to risk, and you don't know what the payoff will be or even if there will be one.

While I had been thusly cogitating, Susannah had been ordering, and the appearance of a fresh margarita and a tangy bowl of homemade salsa snapped me out of my introspection. I sampled both while Susannah told me about her meeting with Srinivasa Patel. It had gone more smoothly than my meeting with Betty but had also ended in ambiguity.

She told me Patel had a doctorate in mathematics and she knew I would be disappointed his concentration was in probability. He had come to the States to take a job at the University of New Mexico teaching math but was currently on a leave of absence doing something for the State based on his expertise in probability and gaming theory. Even though he worked for the University, he knew nothing about their fund-raising operation and had never donated any money to them. He had explained again that he received his invitation to the Ranch by telephone and had accepted it because he thought it would be fun to see a ranch and be up in the mountains. He had no idea why he had been invited, but he hadn't questioned it because he was not familiar with how universities work in the States and figured maybe they periodically held such events for their employees.

That's what she found out for me and my investigation. For herself, she found out that he was single and that his olive skin and white teeth were even more attractive in candlelight. She had arranged for their meeting to be a dinner at Geronimo's in Santa Fe because even though he still had his apartment in Albuquerque, he was staying at the Residence Inn in Santa Fe, courtesy of the taxpayers, while he worked for a government agency.

"Who paid?" I asked, mindful of the cost of an evening at Geronimo's.

"I put it on my expense account," she said and handed me a copy of her receipt.

"Whit didn't say anything about an expense account."

"Well, you better let him know we need one. I'm not driving all the way to Santa Fe on my own nickel, and I'm not driving back on an empty stomach. Besides, if you're trying to get information out of someone, why not ply them with good food and drink? And while I was in Santa Fe, I brought you some of that chile chocolate you like. They sell it at Collected Works."

"A bookstore sells chocolate?"

"Bookstores will sell anything these days. They have to because e-books are cutting into their sales. You can put the chocolate on the expense account, too."

"Hmm. The dinner at Geronimo's was strictly business?"

"It might as well have been. I flirted with him like crazy, but he seemed immune to my feminine wiles."

"He's from India, Suze. I don't think they date over there. Everything is arranged by the families."

"Yeah? Maybe I could get my father to call his father."

42

Layton Kent, Esquire is the most prominent attorney in Albuquerque, and his wife, Mariella, is reputed to be a descendent of Don Francisco Fernandez de la Cueva Enriquez, *Duque de Alburquerque*. In other words, she is said to be the issue of the man after whom our fair city is named. I have never heard *her* say it. She would not do so even were it true because she has too much class for that, but I care less about her ancestors and more about the fact that she is a knowledgeable collector of traditional Native American pots, and I am her personal dealer.

After verifying that I had a lunch meeting with Layton, the *maitre'd* led me to the table and gave me a napkin and wine list. I ordered a bottle of Gruet *Blanc De Noir*. The supercilious sommelier raised his eyebrows and looked to Layton who nodded slightly.

Layton is six inches taller than my 5' 6" and you don't have to be a math whiz to figure that puts him at an even six feet. Calculating his weight is more of a challenge. I place it at around two ninety, but he is surprisingly nimble, has only one chin, and looks rather regal, perhaps like Henry VII without the beard. Also, Mariela is his first and only wife.

"I have allowed you to select the champagne," he said to me, "because I am intrigued by the matter you hinted at over the phone.

And also because you are paying, and even I lack the *chutzpah* to order my usual at your expense."

His usual is Dom Perignon. I have tasted it on occasion at his expense. It is marginally better than Gruet, but certainly not worth six times the expense even if it does deserve to be called champagne because it comes from Champagne and has that *terroir* thing.

The sommelier returned and - although I had ordered and was paying for the bubbly - said, "Shall I pour, Mr. Kent?"

"Yes, Phillip, please."

Layton sipped and indicated his satisfaction with a nod. After the sommelier departed, Layton took another rather larger sip and looked at me. "Most satisfactory."

The waiter arrived and announced that the chef was suggesting elk medallions with juniper sauce and I almost choked on my Gruet. Layton accepted the chef's suggestion for us both. I was not consulted.

After the waiter departed, Layton leaned back in his chair, laced his fingers on the mound of his belly, narrowed his eyes, and asked me to tell him about the pot and how I had come to possess it.

I told him the whole story, leaving nothing out since he is my attorney and anything I tell him is privileged information.

When I finished, he closed his eyes, either to digest what I had said or to take a nap. I couldn't tell which. I studied his suit. He has them hand tailored, perhaps because he likes fine clothes or perhaps because he doesn't like the styles at the big men's shops which are the only places he could buy something off the rack. The one he was wearing that day was of taupe gabardine cut so expertly that it actually made his girth an asset. There was a dark brown handkerchief in the pocket that matched the background color of a tie with rows of small yellow stylized sand cranes. It was knotted over a silk shirt with rolled collar.

I, by contrast, was wearing a cotton shirt from a place on San Mateo, the name of which I can't remember because I buy a shirt only once every five or six years. What I can remember is I paid $12.50 for it. It looked good with the tie my Aunt Beatrice had given me so long ago that its width had actually come back into style.

Layton opened his eyes when the food came, and we both ate in silence except for comments about the food. The elk was better than the one prepared by Maria because it had no doubt never been frozen and was the choice cut, the center of the loin. Maria had been able to offer no side dishes whereas the plate at Layton's club had a purée of gin-marinated green chile and potato and a few leaves of lamb's lettuce allegedly picked wild in the Jemez Mountains. It was an excellent meal, but the juniper sauce was thin, over-salted, and no comparison to Maria's.

Dessert was a *piñon*-scented flan and coffee. Only when that had been consumed did Layton react to what I had told him.

"I will make discreet inquiries to discover if the University knows anything about the pot. I suspect, having dealt with them on numerous occasions, that they do not."

I nodded.

"There is a matter of ethics involved here, Hubert, and I have already thought it through. It is possible that Cyril Duran owns the pot by virtue of being the heir of his great-grandfather. Of course that assumes that the great-grandfather wanted Cyril to have it."

I told him about Martin's theory that I was now the custodian of the pot. A blank stare was all the reply he made. Then I said, "Cyril said his great-grandfather wants the pot back."

His eyes rolled up ever so slightly. "The testimony of spirits is inadmissible. We must also be prepared to fend off any suggestion that the great-grandfather sold or gave the pot to Lawrence."

"Lawrence's letter says the Mexican 'brought' the pot."

"Excellent. That is sufficiently vague for our purposes. When I come into possession of the pot, I am obligated to inform the University, but I need not say how that came about. I will explain to the president that the Taos Pueblo would like the pot repatriated, a request no college president would dare deny these days, and I will point out that the University has no claim to ownership other than the fact that the artifact resided on their property for an extended period. He will no doubt assent to my request. In return for my assistance in this matter, you will

172 The Pot Thief Who Studied D. H. Lawrence

give to Mariela one of the pots you receive from Cyril. Because she has no old Taos pottery, this will be excellent addition to her collection."

I nodded and smiled. Her collection has been the backbone of my business for many years. But my happiness was tempered by the fact that I had lost along the path to this deal a very valuable pot that had been stolen at the Ranch and one of the three Dulcineas I was to receive from Cyril Duran. But two Dulcineas constitute a small fortune, and I had hopes of recovering the lost Anasazi.

43

When I got home, I switched from shank's mule to a Bronco and drove up into the suburban wasteland of northeast Albuquerque to an upscale condo development near the foot of the Sandias.

Teodoro Vasquez was waiting for me and showed me proudly around his place. The kitchen, living room, and dining nook were on the ground floor, and an open staircase led upstairs to a front and rear bedroom. The front one with its dramatic view of the lights of Albuquerque had been converted into what Vasquez called his "command center." A large desk looked westward across the city, and on its surface was a multi-line telephone with an array of buttons, a fax machine, both a desktop and a laptop computer, and the usual assortment of paperclips, pens, pencils, and other office consumables.

The walls were covered with photographs of Vasquez mugging for the camera with the rich and famous. I recognized the last three Governors, our two senators who had been in office as long as I can remember, our representatives whose names I couldn't recall, and a number of others who wore the satisfied expression of people who know they are somebody.

I am nobody, but Teodoro gave me the grand tour nonetheless, and he went through all the pictures, each of which had a funny story behind it, a story that cast a favorable light on Teodoro despite how earnestly he downplayed his part in the tale.

He pointed me to what he called his "client chair" and then swiveled around his yacht of a desk chair and settled into it. He pushed it back and said he had talked with the Head of the State Police after my call and had received permission to share with me everything he knew about the events of the previous weekend at the Lawrence Ranch.

I didn't know why he felt it necessary to consult with the State Police, but I just nodded when he told me he had done so.

"I told Larry," he said (Larry was the Head of the State Police), "that I had urged everyone to call the authorities right from the beginning."

"Indeed you did," I agreed, "and you remained steadfast on that issue."

"I'm glad you remember. Also, I thought we shouldn't move any of the bodies."

"Yes, I distinctly remember you saying that."

"So what can I do you for," he said, probably out of habit because he wasn't the sort to pass up a corny phrase.

"Are you a donor to the University?"

The question seemed to take him aback. A smile even larger than normal formed on his face and he jerked his head to the left and brought it back again quickly in a movement that was neither a nod nor a shake.

"Well," he said, and pushed even further back into his chair. Then he gave a little leg whip to push the chair forward again and leaned forward on his elbows to assume a straightforward look.

And after all that buying of time, the best he could come up with was, "It depends on what you mean by a donation."

"I guess what I mean is did you ever write them a check?"

"A check. Well, no, I don't think so."

"Did you ever allow them to charge a monetary donation to a credit card?"

"Hmm. Not that I recall."

"Maybe you signed over stocks or bonds to them?"

"No, I never play the markets – too risky."

I wondered what other sort of donation there was. Did he take them some old furniture as if they were the Salvation Army?

I just looked at him with a noncommittal expression and waited.

"What I've done on occasion," he finally said, "is to advance their interests in the Legislature. Behind the scenes of course."

"You're not their official lobbyist?"

"No, the University is not on my client list. Everyone on my list gets the best representation money can buy, and you can't do that and take on everybody," he said, making it sound as if the University had sought his assistance and he had turned them down.

"So I suppose they knew you had done that, and that's why they invited you to the Ranch?"

He seemed to be thinking it over carefully, wondering what he could say that couldn't be checked or contradicted.

"Actually," he admitted, "the University isn't aware of what I did for them to help them get a larger appropriation. Just between you and me, if my paying clients knew I was assisting the University *pro bono*, they might not understand."

"Of course. How did your invitation come about?"

"It was a telephone call."

"From?"

"I actually don't remember the name. I'm sure you can appreciate that I get hundreds of invitation in my line of work."

"Of course you do," I said and thanked him for his time and the tour of his condo.

44

I worked for an accounting firm for a couple of years after I got my BBA from UNM, and I hated every minute of it. The working part, not the getting the BBA part. Actually, I didn't like that much either. It wasn't the accounting. I liked getting all the numbers lined up. It was the schedule. Be there at a certain time, leave at a certain time, finish the project by a certain day, eat lunch at the lunch hour. I'm just not cut out for that.

One of my SAPs (Schuze' Anthropological Premises) is that we humans evolved over millions of years as beings who didn't need a schedule. Indeed, a schedule would have been what anthropologists call survival-negative. We hunted when the game was near and gathered when the berries were ripe. Early humans had no words for breakfast, lunch, or dinner. They did have a word for starvation, and they fended that off by eating when the chance arose.

We slept when we were tired, drank when we were thirsty, and the men had sex with the women whenever the alpha male was away and the women were willing or didn't run fast enough. Our courtship rituals have improved, but most of the other trappings of modern society are detrimental to good physical and mental health. The alarm clock, shift work, and the rolodex have put more men in the grave than all the wars in history.

One reason why shopkeeping suits me so well is that I can set my own hours. I hadn't opened at all on Thursday, and now most of Friday had lapsed with the closed sign staring out at the world. It was not yet three when I left Vasquez, and I should have opened the shop because there might have been a customer waiting for me, but in keeping with my anthropological theory, I didn't open because I didn't feel like opening. Of course being true to my theory was made somewhat easier by the knowledge that a substantial sum of money would be coming from the pots I would get from Duran, minus the one I would give to Mariella.

The phone rang and I almost didn't answer it, but I was glad I did. It was Susannah telling me she couldn't meet me at five because she had a date with Patel, and I was happy for her and wished her a pleasant evening. I guess her flirting paid off after all.

Then, since I couldn't think of anything else to do, I opened the shop and found there was indeed someone waiting for me, but it wasn't a customer.

45

She smiled up at me, and at my height how many people can I say that about?

With her pursed lips and turned up nose, she looked a little like a pig. I know that sounds terrible, but I didn't think of it that way. She wasn't like a muddy pig in a barnyard. She was like a cute little pig in a cartoon, like Porky's girlfriend, Petunia.

Except her name was Maria, and she wasn't pink. She was the color of honey when the sun shines through it, and her hair was shiny black and coarse and just long enough to lay down, like a lady Marine who just finished boot camp and whose hair is starting to grow back after being shaved off. And that was good because it showed her cute little ears and her perfectly shaped neck.

She had a large bag slung over her shoulder.

"*Daanzho,*" I said and stood there staring at her.

"You know Apache?"

"You just heard half my vocabulary."

I guess I was still staring at her.

"Are you happy to see me?" she asked.

"Sure."

"Then why don't you invite me in?"

She looked around the shop in awe. "Wow! This is the best collection of pots I've ever seen. Where did you get them?"

"Oh, here and there." I didn't know how she might feel about the Archaeological Resources Protections Act.

"You don't have any baskets."

You often see *jicama* in grocery stores these days because of our growing Hispanic population. '*Jicarilla*' is from the same root with the diminutive ending. Thus, it means something like 'little gourd' or 'little tuber'. The Spanish gave that name to a band of Apaches whose baskets had the shape of gourds. The *Jicarilla*s have some great potters now, but their history is in baskets.

"No, I deal only in pots."

"Don't you like baskets?"

"Sure, but, see, I'm a potter myself. I make pots. But I don't know anything about baskets."

"Maybe you could start making baskets, too."

"Maybe," I said, although after all the years I had spent becoming an expert on Indian pottery, I thought the suggestion was akin to 'Gee, Mister Ma, maybe you could start playing the saxophone along with the cello'.

I took her back to my workshop and showed her where I make pots, and she asked about the clays, the glazes, the wheel, and other things in the shop. She seemed genuinely interested, not just making small talk.

She told me she had business in Albuquerque and decided at the spur of the moment to drop by, and I said I was glad she had and did she want something to eat. She said ever since she became a caterer, she didn't enjoy restaurants. I offered to cook for her, and she liked that idea.

I had a whole chicken in the fridge (a hen, not a rooster), and I used my kitchen shears to cut out the backbone. I put a long piece of aluminum foil in a roasting pan, flattened the chicken out on the foil, covered it with some tomatilla salsa I'd made a few days earlier, folded the rest of the foil over the chicken, placed two bricks on the foil to hold the chicken flat and placed it in the oven. Then I cut up some potatoes and mixed them in a large bowl with a little corn oil, chopped rosemary, ground cumin, and a pinch of kosher salt.

I washed my hands and grabbed two glasses from the fridge. I was reaching for a chilled bottle of Gruet *Blanc de Noir* when she pulled a bottle of Gruet rosé from her bag. "This is a little gift for you," she said and gave me a too-brief kiss. I suspected her visit was not spur-of-the-moment.

I don't like pink champagne, but I accepted it gracefully, took the phone off the hook, and invited Maria out to the patio to sip the sparkling rosé.

She was delighted to see my animal. "What's his name?"

"Geronimo," I said, hoping she wouldn't be offended that he was named after an Apache. But she just laughed and said I have a great sense of humor, because the last thing in the world my dog looked like was a warrior, and she gave me another brief kiss.

The taste was of strawberries, sour cherries, pomegranates and raspberries. That was the Gruet. Maria tasted like lemon and lavender. The Gruet was drier than expected but still had a hint of sweetness. So did Maria. And she knew her sparkling wines. I was beginning to change my mind about rosé.

It was a clear desert night with a warm breeze rustling the chamisa bushes softly against the adobe wall. A shooting star arced across the southern sky, and I thought of Ella Fitzgerald singing *Stars fell on Albuquerque*:

> I can't forget the glamour
> Your eyes held a tender light
> And stars fell on Albuquerque
> That night
>
> I never planned in my imagination
> A situation so heavenly
> A fairy land where no one else could enter
> And in the center just you and me

O.K., the original version has the stars falling on Alabama, but what's romantic about that? And besides that, Carla Glain was in Alabama in my memory drive.

Maria and I, on the other hand, were enclosed in my patio, truly "a fairy land where no one else could enter," and it was a perfect night for romance.

She asked, "What's the other Apache word you know?"

"*Hactcin.*"

"If you only know two words, 'hello' and 'spirit' are good ones to know."

"Maybe you could teach me some more."

"I've forgotten a lot of it. My mother and I moved to Taos when I was eight."

I was thinking as an anthropologist about a story I read about Korean adoptees. One who had been brought to the United States at the age of 8 had kept a diary in Korean for the first few months, but by the time she was twenty, she could remember only three Korean words. I thought the story must be false. Maybe the Korean girl was in an orphanage where she wasn't spoken to often and had delayed language development. I just couldn't believe that you could lose a language you spoke for the first eight years of your life.

"Did you speak Apache growing up?"

"Not much. Like I told you at the Ranch, my mother was Navajo, so she and my father spoke in English."

"Did you ever ask them why?"

She smiled. "Apache children are not allowed to ask why. The elders will tell you things when it is time for you to know them. But it was easy to figure out. My father didn't speak Navajo and my mother didn't speak Apache, so English was the only option. But at least she tried to learn some Apache because we were living in Dulce."

"Why did she move to Taos?"

She smiled again.

"I know," I said, "you didn't ask."

"I didn't have to. She told me she and my father were getting a divorce. My father and I were never close, so it didn't bother me. But his father – my grandfather – was my favorite person. He's the one who taught me what Apache I learned. He used to say the children were the future of the tribe, and I needed to learn to talk. That was the phrase he used, 'learn to talk' – like English wasn't talking. He made me feel important. He came to see me in Taos every weekend. When he met the man I was going to marry, he asked me if I was sure. I said yes, and he nodded. I should have read him better. The marriage lasted about three months. My father didn't come to the wedding, but my grandfather did. I still miss him."

I thought of Cyril Duran. "Does his spirit talk to you?"

"Yes, in my dreams."

I excused myself to take the chicken out to rest. I switched the oven to broil, slid the potatoes onto a cookie sheet and under the flame, and chopped some fresh cilantro to go over the chicken. When the potatoes were done, I cut the chicken into two halves and placed each one on a plate with the potatoes.

I offered her a choice of dining at my table or outside, and she chose a romantic meal under the stars. The rosé was gone so I opened a bottle of *Blanc de Noir*. I sipped slowly, mindful of what wine can do to an old rooster. Geronimo nuzzled up to Maria and was rewarded with several pieces of chicken and a few potatoes. He's an omnivore.

I was all out of chocolate, so after dinner I told her I didn't know what we could do about dessert, and she said, "We'll think of something" and ran her tongue across her small perfect mouth and kissed me with enthusiasm.

I put my arms around her and slid my hands under her blouse. Her back felt warm and firm. We kissed for a very long time. Ella ran through a couple more stanzas during that kiss. Then Maria led me inside being careful to make Geronimo stay in the patio. I started to kiss her again, but she pushed me away, stepped back and took off her blouse. Then her bra. Then her... well, you see where this is leading. She took off everything down to and including little footlets off her cute little feet while I stood there mesmerized.

I thought about my belief that you really should get to know a woman before jumping into bed with her, but with each piece of clothing that hit the floor, I felt I knew her better. What the hell, we'd spent a weekend together at the Ranch and an entire evening in my patio. That should qualify as knowing her well enough.

It finally dawned on me that the operation she had in mind would go more smoothly if I too disrobed, and I was lifting a hand to the top button of my shirt when Susannah barged in.

46

"Hubie, thank God you're here. Something's happened to Srini."

Susannah is strong and steady, and although there was terror in her big brown eyes, she was keeping it under control. She looked over at Maria and said, "Hi Maria. Sorry to interrupt."

Maria pulled a sheet off my bed and wrapped it around herself. I asked Susannah what had happened.

"We went back to his apartment after dinner, but after we got inside, he remembered something in his car and went outside. When he didn't come back, I went out to see what happened, and he was gone."

"Was his car still there?"

"Yes." She started trembling. "But there was blood on the trunk lid. I called you from Srini's phone, but I kept getting a busy signal."

"It's off the hook."

She looked at Maria. "I guess I know why."

"How did you get here?"

"I drove my car to Srini's place, and we took his to the restaurant. When you didn't answer your phone, I came over in my car."

I turned to Maria.

"I'll watch Geronimo until you get back," she said.

I gave her a brief kiss. Susannah and I ran out to the Bronco. She gave me directions to the apartment and showed me the blood when we got there. I was trying to figure out what to do when Srini walked out of his apartment with a bloody towel on his head. The way he had it wound around his head made him look like a Sikh except without the beard.

"Srini!" Susannah cried and ran to him. "Are you alright? What happened?"

"I bent over to open the boot and someone hit me on the head. Thank God I have a thick skull! I turned to see someone running into the darkness, and I followed."

"Why would you do that?" asked Susannah.

"To apprehend my assailant," he said as if everyone runs after attackers. "I chased the blackguard for several blocks, but lost him."

"Are you badly hurt?"

"I don't know."

I asked him to move the towel and Susannah and I looked at the wound. There was a lot of blood and the area seemed dented. I was afraid he had a cracked skull and suggested we call an ambulance. He tried to resist but Susannah placed the call.

I asked Patel some questions about his work with the State, specifically which agency he was working for and what it had to do with his specialty in probability.

After Susannah finished the 911 call, she objected to my questioning Patel. I reminded her it's standard procedure to keep people with people head injuries talking to prevent them lapsing into a coma. But that wasn't my only motive for questioning him.

The ambulance crew let Susannah ride inside with Srini. I stood there watching the flashing red lights disappear around the corner.

Then I remembered Maria. I drove back home to find a note saying Geronimo had gone to sleep and she was on her way back to Taos to do the same.

C'est amour.

47

What with the excitement of Maria shedding her clothes and Srini being attacked, I was too revved up to sleep. I figured reading Lawrence would make me drowsy, so I started *The Man Who Died*.

I estimate I've read around ten thousand books, but *The Man Who Died* had to rank as one of the weirdest. It begins with the title character waking up in the tomb. He then "slowly followed the road away from the town, past the olives, under which purple anemones were drooping in the chill of dawn, and rich-green herbage was pressing thick. The world, the same as ever, the natural world, thronging with greenness, a nightingale winsomely, wistfully, coaxingly calling from the brushes beside a runnel of water, in the world, the natural world of morning and evening, forever undying, from which he had died."

I figured with turgid prose like that, I'd be nodding off after a few pages, but something about the story kept me reading. I'll spare you most of the details, the majority of which involve convoluted descriptions of the sort quoted above. The man ends up in Lebanon where he meets a virgin of twenty-seven who has been lusted after by all manner of men including Caesar and Anthony. She has built a temple to Isis and devoted herself to tending the temple and engaging in worship. She has asked a philosopher, "Are all women born to be given to men?"

The philosopher answers, "Rare women wait for the re-born man." It's a moment of lucidity in Lawrence's prose, a simple declarative sentence whose meaning is clear without being heavy-handed. The woman in the temple is the "rare woman" and the man who died is the "re-born man."

But he couldn't let it alone, because he has the philosopher continue: "For the lotus, as you know, will not answer to all the bright heat of the sun. But she curves her dark, hidden head in the depths, and stirs not. Till, in the night, one of these rare invisible suns that have been killed and shine no more, rises among the stars in unseen purple, and like the violet, sends its rare, purple rays out into the night."

I'm just a humble potter, but I'm not so naïve as to believe that Lawrence was really talking about lotuses and violets. His descriptions are like Georgia O'Keeffe's paintings. One is describing flowers and the other is painting them, but their works are not about flowers. They are about sex.

But so what? It's not erotic. It's not even titillating. It's just boring. Lawrence took all the fun out of sex by philosophizing it in murky prose. At least O'Keeffe's paintings are beautiful to look at. But I'm neither a literary critic nor an art critic, just a humble artisan who works in clay.

As you have no doubt already guessed, the man who died makes love to the woman of the temple.

I thought about O'Keeffe's painting of the tree I had seen in front of the Lawrence cabin. She came to New Mexico five years after Lawrence left and spent several weeks at the Ranch where she painted the giant pine. O'Keeffe wrote that she would lie under the tree and stare into the branches. The tree in her painting, *The Lawrence Tree*, doesn't look much like the one I saw, but I wasn't lying down when I saw it, and I was on the verge of frostbite, so it's little wonder that she saw it differently. Indeed, she saw everything differently. When she taught at West Texas State Normal College in Canyon, she used to walk out to Palo Duro Canyon and paint landscapes.

When she showed one to a local resident, he said, "That doesn't look like the canyon."

"I painted it the way I felt," she replied.

"You must have had a stomach ache," he said.

48

"It's called *The Man Who Died*, and it's about a guy back in Roman times leaving his tomb and wandering around until he ends up in Lebanon where he has sex with a woman who tends a temple devoted to Isis."

Susannah took a sip of her margarita and said, "That makes sense."

"It does?"

"Sure. She must have taken the risen guy to be Osiris."

"How did you know that?"

"We study all that in art history. I must have seen dozens of paintings and statues of Isis and Osiris. And we have to know the stories behind the images. See, Osiris was a pharaoh loved by his people and Isis was his sister and his wife."

I frowned.

"The Egyptian royalty were even more inbred than the European royalty," she explained. "Anyway, his brother was jealous, so he took Osiris' measurements while he was asleep and had a jeweled casket made exactly to those measurements. Then the brother threw a big party where he brought out the casket and announced he would give it to anyone for whom it was an exact fit, sort of like Cinderella except I like the glass slipper better than a coffin. Anyway, all the guests tried it on for size, but none of them fit. Then Osiris got in and it was perfect for him. But the evil brother slammed the lid shut, sealed it with molten lead, and tossed it into the Nile."

"Sort of like Cain and Abel," I mused. "I think brother stories like that are found in every society."

"But this one has a romantic ending, Hubie. Isis loved Osiris madly, so she searched for his casket everywhere. She finally found it and brought it back for a decent burial. But the evil brother discovered it and chopped the body into pieces which he scattered throughout Egypt. But Isis didn't give up. She started searching for the parts of her husband. Eventually she found all the parts except one and reassembled Osiris and wrapped him in bandages. Was the guy from the tomb wrapped in bandages?"

"He was."

"See? It had to be Osiris. Now here's the strange part. After Isis puts Osiris back together again, she breathed life back into him and Osiris made love to her."

"What's so strange about that? The guy obviously hadn't had sex in quite a while, being sealed up in a casket."

She gave me that enigmatic smile she does so well. "Remember I said Isis didn't find *all* of his parts? There was one missing."

She sat there smiling at me.

"His..." I started but hesitated about what word to use.

"Uh huh," she said.

"Then how could they make love?"

"That's the romantic part, Hubie. I guess they loved each other so much that it didn't matter. She even got pregnant and gave birth to Horus who eventually killed the evil brother. But in that fight, Horus lost an eye, and his one eye became a famous Egyptian symbol called the 'all-seeing eye'. That's the eye in the pyramid on our dollar bills."

"You made that up."

"I didn't. You can look it up. Now, did Lawrence ever say who the man who died actually was?"

"He never gave him a name. At first I thought it was Jesus because it was during Roman times, he was in a tomb and he came out alive."

"It was Jesus, Hubie. It's like an allegory. Horus was an immaculate conception. So was Jesus. The man who died arose from a tomb. So did Jesus. And when the Jesus character in the story has sex with the woman in the temple, it's an analogy with Isis and Osiris. In both cases, they didn't have real physical sex."

I thought back on Lawrence's words. "No Suze, I don't think it was an analogy." I pulled the book out of my pocket, found the passage I wanted, and read, "He crouched to her, and he felt the blaze of his manhood and his power rise up in his loins."

"Then guess what he says," I asked her.

She looked slightly flustered. "I have no idea," she said.

"Lawrence has the man who died say at that moment, 'I am risen!'."

"Wow! No wonder they banned his books!"

49

The next morning over coffee, the solution to the murders came to me as I was thinking about *And Then There Were None* and *The Man Who Died*.

Isn't literature great?

I made some phone calls then visited a costume shop where I was amazed by the merchandise and assisted by the owner.

Then I explained my theory to Whit and went to the University with him to meet with some of the staff from the fund-raising office where his badge helped expedite getting the information I needed.

I asked him if he could round up all the people we needed for a meeting the next evening and he said with the cooperation of the State Police, he could round up anybody I named, and that proved to be almost true. Only one person on my list declined to show, and when Whit asked me if he should force the issue, I said no.

Cyril Duran came to my shop that afternoon. I placed his great-grandfather's pot on the counter. He cupped it in his hands and closed his eyes. He said a few words in *Tewa*, but I didn't catch enough of it to make sense.

"Thank you," he said when he had finished his recitation.

I put a cardboard box on the counter, wrapped the pot in bubblewrap, placed it in the box and filled the box with Styrofoam peanuts. Cyril walked out with it.

I assumed he would be back, but I didn't know if it would be that day, next month, or next year. I found my place in the book about zero, which sounds better than calling it a book about nothing, and started reading.

He returned about an hour later with a box of his own from which he extracted three beautiful Taos pots from the early 20th Century.

"How did you come to be named Cyril?"

"My brother and me were named by a priest from Eastern Europe."

"Your brother's name is Methodius?"

"Yes." He smiled. "I guess I'm the lucky one."

"The priest is the one who told you about me?"

I took his silence as a yes.

"See you around," he said as he left.

So he really was opportunity after all. And sent from heaven. Well, sent by Father Groas, which is about as close to heaven as I get.

I studied Dulcinea's pots. They were well-formed and symmetrical. They were burnished smoothly in a fashion impossible without a wheel. They were perfect except for the fact that they lacked soul. I thought about the potter whose works I had unearthed in that summer dig so many years ago, and I asked her what she thought.

"They are not us," she said.

What the hell. If Cyril Duran's great-grandfather can speak to him, why can't a tenth century potter speak to me?

50

The next evening found me standing in front of my counter and looking at eighteen people, some curious and some furious. I looked at the crowd and thought to myself that if I could attract this many customers to my shop, I could be rich.

But they weren't customers. Srinivasa Patel was on the front row of borrowed chairs from *Dos Hermanas*, still looking like a Sikh without a beard, except the towel had been replaced by a bandage. Susannah was sitting next to him, looking at him adoringly. Carl Wron was next to Betty Shanile. Layton Kent was at the end of the row.

Teodoro Vasquez was sitting in the second row next to a man who looked like the villain in a Hollywood thriller. He had a face like a hatchet, dark shifty eyes, and acne-scarred cheeks. I had never seen him before.

Seated next to him was another man I had never seen before. A burly guy with curly hair, he looked like a model you might see in those outdoorsy clothes in the L. L. Bean Catalog. A book stuck out of both of his coat pockets.

Fred Givens was in the next chair, and Chauncey Benthrop was seated to his right. Neither one of them looked like anyone you would see in a movie or a catalog. Tristan had the last seat on the row.

The third row held Bob Saunders, Howard Glover, the man we all knew as Don Canon and Adele the Serving Wench.

There were also two uniformed policemen in the crowd.

Whit Fletcher leaned over to me and said, "That dame with the food ain't gonna show up again is she?" I told him I couldn't stop her, but we'd reached a compromise – Gladys wouldn't come until I signaled her by turning out the outside light over the door. He groaned but accepted it and walked to the back and stood behind the two men in blue.

Then he nodded to me, and I started with the line I can't resist in such situations. "You're probably wondering why I called you all together," I said, and Fletcher rolled his eyes, Susannah sighed and Tristan laughed.

"Most of you were at the Lawrence Ranch with me. It was an event none of us will ever forget because three people were murdered."

"I still don't think we can be certain of that," said Teodoro Vasquez.

"My client has no knowledge regarding the causes of death of the three persons you refer to," said the man seated next to him.

"Who are you?" asked Fletcher.

"I am Dalton Figg, Mr. Vasquez' attorney." When he spoke, his hatchet face elongated and his incisors protruded over his lower lip. I thought of Mae West's quip that his mother should have thrown him away and kept the stork.

Layton Kent made a slight puffing noise as if expelling something unpleasant from his mouth.

"I don't believe Mr. Vasquez had anything to do with the deaths," I reassured Figg.

The pettifogger's incisors retreated and he looked around the room with a satisfied expression as if he had just accomplished something.

"As Mr. Vasquez has reminded us," I continued, "there was some question, even to the very end, whether the deaths were murders or accidents. However, forensic examinations have been completed on all three victims, and they all died from a blow to the back of the skull."

Srini's eyes widened and Susannah shuddered.

"Fred Rich was dead before he was placed in a tub of icy water, Charles Winant was unconscious before he was placed in the freezer, and we all saw Carla Glain on the floor of her room."

Fred Givens lowered his head.

"In order to understand what happened up in the mountains north of Taos, we first have to understand why we were all there to begin with. The fund-raising office at the University periodically holds events to which they invite past, current, and prospective donors. They decided to hold such an event at the Lawrence Ranch, and they invited a number of current or would-be donors. The distinguished silver-haired gentleman standing at the back of the room is Detective First Grade Whit Fletcher from the Albuquerque Police Department."

"Cut the crap, Hubert, and get on with it."

I did. "Detective Fletcher has a list of all the people invited to the event in question. Twelve people originally accepted, but as the event neared, the weather forecast was ominous. The University decided to cancel the event and began calling the confirmed invitees to let them know. They reached eight of the twelve people. The four they did not reach were Betty Shanile, Robert Saunders, Carl Wron, and Howard Glover, all of whom showed up at the ranch not knowing the event had been cancelled. They are all here today."

"It's not all that surprising that four out of twelve people could not be reached on such short notice. What is surprising is that six other people showed up who are not on the original list that detective Fletcher obtained from the University. Those six were Fred Rich, Charles Winant, Carla Glain, Srinivasa Patel, Teodoro Vasquez, and Agatha Cruz. The obvious question is why were *they* there?"

"My client," said Figg, rising from his chair as if to lodge an objection in court, "received a proper invitation and cannot be held responsible for any errors made by the University."

"Mr. Figs," said Fletcher, "we're here to find out what happened, and it'll go a lot smoother if you'll just stay quiet and let Mr. Schuze here explain it for us."

"It's Figg, not Figs."

"I don't care if it's peaches. Just sit down and shut up."

"My client has a constitutional right to representation," he stammered, his incisors making another unscheduled public appearance.

"Your client has not been charged with anything," said Layton. "This is a private meeting in Mr. Schuze' home. If you insist on interrupting our host, he has the right to have you put off the premises."

"And the means," added Fletcher.

Figg sat down and I continued.

"All three of the murder victims came from the group of five who were not on the University's original list. For ease of reference, I'll just call them the non-donors."

If you noticed that I said 'five' when the number started out as 'six', then you are paying more attention than the people in my shop were. They didn't notice. I changed the number for a reason you will come to understand.

I continued, "Since there were four donors from the official list and five non-donors not on that list, you can calculate the probability that all three victims were—"

"Come on, Hubie," pleaded Susannah. "Don't do the math. Just give us the odds."

"The odds against all three victims coming from the non-donors are approximately six to one."

"Them ain't very good odds," Fletcher noted, "but a few people beat them every day at the roulette wheels."

I pointed out that someone had attacked Patel and since the *modus operandi* of that attack was the same as in the case of the first three victims – a blow to the back of the head – we had to assume he was supposed to be victim number four, and that raised the odds to ten to one.

"You still can't take it to court," said Fletcher.

"True," I agreed, "but it was enough to make me start wondering what the five people had in common. Carla Glain struck me as the sort of person likely to have little in common with the others, so I started with her. What I learned from Fred Givens and her other co-workers was more or less what I expected. She was an intense person who had few interests outside of her work. She was unmarried, didn't travel and didn't even take all the vacations days she had coming to her. Indeed, I couldn't imagine her attending the event at the Ranch, but Mr. Givens explained it to me."

I looked at him. He cleared his throat and said, "She wasn't going to go, but I talked her into it. I feel terrible about that. She had just been appointed to the Gaming Commission by the new Governor, and that's a pretty prestigious appointment, so I told her that was probably why she received the invitation. She didn't want to disappoint the Governor, so she decided to go. If I had just kept my mouth shut, she might still be—"

"You did what seemed right at the time," I told him. "If we avoided all actions that might turn out to have unforeseen consequences, we wouldn't be able to do anything, and our inaction would also have consequences. In my own case, I regret not following up on the fact that Carla had been appointed to the Gaming Commission. Had I done so, the attack on Mr. Patel might have been avoided. I'm just lucky the attack led to nothing more than a headache."

"I am even more fortunate," piped up Patel.

"But I did eventually put it together. I remembered Charles Winant expressed a profound dislike of gambling when we met. I knew from Fred Givens that Carla Glain was on the Gaming Commission. And while waiting for the ambulance to arrive, Mr. Patel told me he was working for the Gaming Commission helping them understand games of chance. He has a doctorate in mathematics with a specialty in probability theory. Yesterday morning I called the Gaming Commission and learned that Carla Glain was not the only new member appointed by the new Governor. There were two others – Fred Rich and Charles Winant."

A collective gasp issued forth from the audience. It was an exciting moment, and I felt a little rush at having delivered the dramatic news. I don't know exactly how to describe the feeling I had. The Germans probably have a word for it like *weltanschauung* or *schadenfreude* or something like that.

51

The collective gasp was followed by a knock at the door. It was Miss Gladys Claiborne, rapping my door with one hand and balancing a tray about the size of a small trampoline with the other.

"I thought she wasn't coming until you signaled her, Hubert," protested Fletcher.

I raised my shoulders, dropped them, and went and opened the door.

"Lordy, I do believe I'm about to lose this tray. Would you be so kind as to help me with this, Detective Fletcher?" He started to say something, but she lurched forward and he grabbed the tray. She looked at him admiringly. "You are light on your feet for such a big man. Now, Mr. Schuze, you grab this side…perfect, and I'll just say a few words to your guests."

As we walked back towards the counter, I told Whit the outside light burned out. Evidently the bulb had emitted its last lumen just moments before my dramatic announcement about Rich and Winant, and Miss Gladys must have been standing at the ready by her door, tray in hand.

While we unloaded the tray onto my counter, Miss Gladys turned her round creamy face and its small blue eyes to the group and said, "Mr. Schuze doesn't entertain often, and he never remembers to provide the little snacks that make any gathering a success. Well, they say the Lord moves in mysterious ways, and you just have to believe it's true, because I'm his neighbor and I just adore making party food, so it works out well for everyone, doesn't it?"

She walked over to the counter and looked down at the layout of the dishes disapprovingly and then rearranged them. "What I've brought," she said, pointing to each one as she named it, "is festive sausage balls, shrimp-stuffed mushrooms, bacon cheese puffs, barbequed cocktail franks, broiled BBQ wings with blue cheese dipping sauce, bourbon honey chicken thighs, and that old stand-by, deviled eggs. For your sweet tooth, I've brought spiced pecans, little squares of Coca-Cola cake – that was one of Mr. Claiborne's favorite – and brownies."

Some people got up to make a selection while Fletcher just stood there shaking his head. When Miss Gladys saw that others were remaining in their chairs, she put a few selections back on the tray and carried it back to them. Adele the Serving Wench just turned her head. One of the policemen reached for a sausage ball.

Miss Gladys brought the tray back to the counter, and I selected a bourbon honey chicken thigh. It was sweet, crispy, gooey and delicious. I had another. Whit gave in and picked up a barbequed cocktail frank. Somehow I knew that's what he would choose.

"Now that we've had something to eat," I suggested, "we should all return to our seats." They all did so with a little prodding from Fletcher, and I returned to my explanation.

"It cannot be a coincidence that Carla Glain, Fred Rich, and Charles Winant were all new appointees to the Gaming Commission and all ended up at the Ranch. Nor can it be a coincidence that the two other people of the non-donor group also have ties to the Commission. As I mentioned, Mr. Patel is working for them, and it turns out that Mr. Vasquez is the lobbyist for Citizens for Responsible Gaming, a pro-gambling group."

"That isn't accurate," said Vasquez. "CFRG was established to insure that New Mexicans can maintain the right to play games of chance, and we educate them on how to do that responsibly."

"Wording chosen so as to qualify the group as an educational organization so it won't have to register under the lobbying laws," observed Layton Kent.

Figg rose again and said, "CFRG is a perfectly legal organization formed—"

"Sit down, Figs," commanded Fletcher.

He sat.

I continued. "Three questions remain. First, who invited the five people with ties to gaming? Second, why did someone start trying to kill them all? Third, who did it?"

"We all know who did it," said Adele the Serving Wench. "It was that creepy old woman, Agatha Cruz." A number of people nodded their agreement.

"We'll come to her in a minute," I said. "But let's go through the questions as I listed them. First, who invited the non-donors? Mr. Canon?"

The man we all knew as Don Canon looked at me calmly but did not move or speak. He was turning out to be, if not unflappable, at least less flappable than I would have guessed. The man who looked like the L. L. Bean model stood up, looked around the room and said, "My name is Don Canon."

It was another Dramatic Moment, and I have to admit I enjoyed it again. It was like that old television show, To Tell the Truth, where one of the three panelists stands up at the end and announces he is the real Dudley Doright. Maybe it was childish on my part, but I really like seeing the looks on their faces. Carl Wron, Betty Shanile, Robert Saunders, and Howard Glover were all glancing back and forth between the man they all knew as Don Canon and the man who was now standing and claiming that name.

The real Don Canon paused to let what he said sink in and then said, "I have a confession to make. On Wednesday night, I got the call that the event was being cancelled, but I was told to stay at the Ranch in case they couldn't reach all the invitees. I didn't want to stay. The reason need not be mentioned here. Mr. Schuze knows what the reason was, and it has nothing to do with what happened at the Ranch. I called an acquaintance of mine, Johnny Carrasco, and asked him if he would fill in for me. He said he couldn't do it, so I thought I was going to be stuck there. But the next morning he called and said he could do it after all. He came up later that day and I left. I got snowed in at Taos like everyone else, and I didn't return to the Ranch until Monday. I spent a couple of days cleaning up, repaired the phone line, took care of the livestock and did some work on the truck. The police talked to me briefly to verify that I had asked Johnny to fill in for me, but they had already searched the place before I returned and they didn't tell me much. We don't get television up there and no papers are delivered, so I didn't know all the details of what had gone on until I got a call from Mr. Schuze yesterday morning. I heard Mr. Schuze tell Mr. Givens that we shouldn't feel guilty about the unintended results of things we do, and obviously I had no idea what would happen after I left, but I still feel terrible about it. Three people are dead who might be alive if I had not left my post."

A hush came over the room, and I let it hang there for a few moments before I called on Johnny Carrasco, the man formerly known to us as Don Canon.

"I also feel bad about what happened," he said. "Like Don said, I told him I couldn't fill in for him when he called me that night. But later that evening I was talking to Agatha Cruz and she said she had a group of people she owed a favor, and it would be great if she could invite them to the Ranch for a free weekend. I told her I wasn't interested in helping her throw a party. I hardly knew the old bag. But she offered to pay me five hundred dollars, and I couldn't turn it down, so I told her to go ahead and call her friends. Then I got my girlfriend, Adele Carlton, to go with me and pretend to be a worker up there because I figured I'd need the help, and I wanted her to be with me anyway. Of course we pretended just to be co-workers because I didn't want to get Don in trouble by having anyone there say something later about how the boss and the waitress were fooling around." He looked around to the others with an earnest expression on his face. "If I had known what that crazy old lady was going to do, I never would have gone up there. I feel bad just like Don."

When Carrasco sat down, everyone turned to me. "It seems that two of the three questions have been answered. We are told that Agatha Cruz invited the non-donors and that she killed them. But the question of why remains unanswered."

"I think you answered it," said Carrasco. "You told us the people she invited all had some connection to gambling. I guess she hated gambling."

"But why would she hate gambling enough to start killing people associated with it? Had her husband squandered the family fortune at the tables? Was she an escapee from a prison for the criminally insane? What do we know about her?"

I asked Fletcher what the State Police had found out about Agatha Cruz.

"They checked NCIC. I guess everyone knows these days because of television that NCIC is the National Crime Information Center. There was no record of anyone with that name. They checked the driving license records for all fifty states and U.S. possessions, and no one with that name has either a drivers license or a state-issued ID. They checked with Social Security, and no one with that name has a Social Security card."

"She must have been using an alias," observed Figg.

"Obviously," I said. "What name did you know her by, Mr. Carrasco?"

"She told me she was Agatha Cruz. I had no reason to doubt her."

"And where did you meet her?"

He shrugged. "I don't remember."

"Well, you said you talked to her last week when she told you she'd pay you five hundred dollars to let her invite some friends to the Ranch. Where did that conversation take place?"

"I ran into her at a bar."

"And you told her about Don wanting you to take his place? Why would you do that?"

"I guess it just sort of came up in the conversation. You know how it is when you're just making small talk."

"You knew her well enough to agree to her proposal?"

"I hardly knew her at all, man. But I know five hundred dollars when I see it."

"I don't doubt you do. But I think the amount of money you received for pretending to be Don Canon was a great deal more than five hundred dollars. Because no one would agree to be an accessory to murder for a paltry five hundred dollars."

"I already told you I feel bad, but I didn't know she was gonna murder anyone, so I'm not an accessory."

"I'll leave that detail to the District Attorney. Detective Fletcher, did the State Police find any trace of Agatha Cruz?"

"She didn't jump off that cliff, if that's what you're asking. There was nothing down there."

I just stood there looking over the heads of the crowd and waiting.

"Wait a minute," said Glover. "We circled the whole building after we found Glain dead and her window open, and the only fresh tracks were the ones between the window and the cliff."

"Right," I said, "and I made the ridiculous suggestion that she might have rappelled down the cliff."

"That was ridiculous," said Susannah, rather gratuitously, I thought.

"And I made the suggestion," said Glover, "that someone might have climbed up the cliff and gone into the room, killed Glain, and carried Cruz back down the cliff. I guess that's a pretty ridiculous suggestion, too." He looked at me. "But it happened some other way didn't it?"

"It did. The person who killed Glain left through the window, walked out to the cliff, then walked back to the window and climbed back into the room. That's why the only tracks were between the window and the cliff. In the soft snow, we couldn't determine which way a print was facing. We just saw mashed down spots more or less the size of a foot."

"It *is* a locked room mystery!" shouted Susannah, and everyone turned to her with puzzled looks. "You know," she said, "when the dead person is found alone in a room and you have to figure out how she was killed. Carla Glain's room was locked. We all heard the bolt slide into place."

"That's right," said Glover, "I had to break down the door."

"Exactly," said Susannah. "So she was killed while she was locked in a room, and the only other person in the room left through the window but came back in and... wait a minute, Hubie. The only other person in the room that night was Agatha Cruz, and she wasn't in there when Howard broke down the door."

"Actually, she was. You remember when it started raining that night? I didn't know whether it was rain, snow, or sleet?"

"Yeah, you had to open the window and stick your hand way out to see which it was."

"Right. When we broke into Glain's room, we saw Agatha's blue robe and pink slippers under the open window."

"And?"

"And they were soaking wet and the floor around them had standing water. But the rain didn't cause that. It was a gentle rain falling straight down, and the windows are protected by deep eaves. That's why I had to reach way out to see what was falling. So the only way the floor below the window could be wet was from the water that came out of the robe and slippers. And the only way the robe and slippers could be that waterlogged would be if someone wore them out into the rain and then came back."

"But then where did she go? Where was she?"

"She must have been hiding under the bed," I answered. "She walked out to the cliff in the robe and slippers to make us think she had jumped. Then she retraced her steps and climbed back in through the window. Then she took off the robe and slippers and left them on the floor. Her bare feet were dry or maybe she ran a dry handkerchief over them just to be sure, but she left no track as she walked over to the bed and slipped underneath it."

"But we never saw her again," said Saunders. "Are you telling us she stayed under the bed all day until the police came and questioned us and everyone went home?"

"Even that wouldn't work," said Glover. "The police searched the room thoroughly. They must have looked under the bed, in the closet, and everywhere else."

"I'm sure they did," I said, "but she had been out of the room for hours by that time. She left as soon as all of us went back to the main room."

"And she hid somewhere else in the building, right, Hubie? I'll bet it was the freezer. No one would ever think to look there. Remember you said she had all that stuff under her gown? I'll bet it was warm clothing so she could hide in the freezer."

"That's a good theory, Suze, but it won't quite work. The police had to go into the freezer to retrieve the two bodies."

"Well, what did she do? Ascend into heaven?"

"No, she just walked out amongst us. Then she said she needed to visit the bathroom, and Benthrop said we shouldn't let her go alone."

Susannah furrowed her brow. "But that was Adele, not Agatha."

"Precisely. Adele Carlton and Agatha Cruz are one and the same person."

52

If you thought the first two big revelations shocked the crowd, you should have seen them this time. They were stunned. This was truly a Dramatic Moment.

Naturally, Adele was the first to speak. I won't call her the Serving Wench any longer because as you can see, she now had a bigger problem than poor customer service.

"That's crazy," was all she said, and looking at the faces in the crowd told me most of them agreed with her.

I looked at Saunders, Glover, Vasquez, Benthrop, Patel, Wron, Shanile and Susannah. "Think back. You never saw the two of them at the same time or place. Whenever Adele Carlton was present, Agatha Cruz was in her room. Whenever Agatha Cruz was present, Adele Carlton was conveniently off duty. You may recall that Cruz was the only one not present when we found Rich's body. After we all gathered in the main room and discussed the situation, I became concerned about Cruz not yet being up, and I asked Don – actually Carrasco –if we should check on her. Instead of doing it himself, he sent Adele to do it."

Glover said, "I remember that because Carla Glain made a remark along the lines that you ask a man to do something and he delegates it to a woman."

"You may also remember that it was at least half an hour before Cruz finally appeared."

"I do remember that. Carl and I went out to cut up the elk and when we finished, she still hadn't made an appearance."

"And when she did," I continued, "her makeup looked hastily applied and there was powder on her blouse."

"I noticed that," said Betty, "but I thought it was just because she was old and maybe couldn't see too well."

"Her glasses were greasy," I noted. "But her hair was perfect. That's because it was a wig."

"This is all ridiculous," said Carrasco. "When Adele wasn't in the big room, she was with me. We were trying to keep our relationship a secret, so naturally she was sneaking around, but you can't honestly believe she can be two people at once."

I had Saunders, Glover, Vasquez, Benthrop, Patel, Wron, Shanile and Susannah almost convinced, but it was a bizarre theory, and I think Carrasco's explanation and his calm demeanor undermined some of the progress I had made. So I pulled a small bottle out of my pocket and dabbed a bit of its contents onto the back of my hand while everyone sat there probably wondering what the devil this idiot was doing now. Then I walked by Saunders, Glover, Vasquez, Benthrop, Patel, Wron, Shanile and Susannah in turn and asked them to take a whiff of my hand, but not to say anything until everyone had smelled it.

When I had finished this little experiment, I asked them what it reminded them of and Patel was the first to speak. "It smells like old Miss Cruz," he said.

"It does," said Susannah. "I was wondering where I had smelled that before."

The next to speak was Betty. She, too, agreed it reminded her of Cruz, and by that time all the others were nodding in agreement.

I held the bottle up for all to see. "This is spirit gum. I just learned yesterday that it's used in the theater to hold on wigs, fake beards, long noses, and other sorts of theatrical prostheses. I bought this bottle at an interesting shop down on Central that sells costumes and theater supplies. It's the same place you bought yours, Ms. Carlton. I had a snapshot of you – taken by a phone of all things – and the owner of the shop identified you by name. It seems you're fairly well known in local theater circles."

She just glared at me. Whit Fletcher told her she had a right to remain silent and all the other things that she had a right to. Then they led her away. They let Carrasco go, and told him he could go back to Taos but no further and that they wanted to question him further in the morning after they had done some more investigating.

53

Everyone else stayed and polished off all the food Miss Gladys had brought. Except for the sugared pecans. I had surreptitiously put most of those in my pocket.

Betty Shanile and Carl Wron were sitting on the front row talking quietly. Susannah, Srini, and Glover were standing off to one side laughing. Fred Givens had been trapped by Benthrop who was holding forth on his theories about the welcome decline of western civilization. Tristan was entertaining Layton Kent who seemed to be enjoying it, and Whit and Miss Gladys were reminiscing about the good old days when the police could put criminals in jail without warnings and warrants and all the other roadblocks the Supreme Court has thrown into the road to justice. Vasquez and his attorney had left.

I was chatting with the real Don Canon. In response to my question, he told me he always carried two books so that if he finished one, he had another to read. I liked him immediately. He also said he was making plans for another event at the Ranch and asked me if I'd be willing to do my pot lecture again. A couple of people had said they liked it. I said I would think about it.

Eventually everyone left except Tristan, and he helped me tidy up the shop. We went back to my living quarters and I opened a bottle of Gruet. Tristan isn't crazy about champagne. I know I shouldn't call it that, but old habits are difficult to break. He helped himself to a Tecate and some tortilla chips. I was having sugared pecans with the bubbly.

"That was quite a performance, Uncle Hubert."

"You really think so?" I think of him almost like a son, and I love it when he's proud of me. How often can we forty-somethings impress the youngsters?

"I like the way you sort of brought everyone along rather than just springing the conclusion. I wish more of the professors would do that. Too many of them like to show off. They spout a lot of theories, but they don't explain why we should accept them. I guess they think we should figure it out on our own or maybe just take their word for it."

"I had some pretty good professors when I was there," I told him. "They did just what you said. They took us along the path one step at a time so that by the time we got to the Big Theory, we knew what it meant and why it was the accepted theory. But maybe the quality of instruction has declined."

"Or maybe I'll look back and think they were better when I'm your age."

Tristan is an insightful lad, I thought to myself.

"Emily said to tell you she was happy you liked finding out about that pot that some guy gave to Lawrence."

I hadn't told Tristan I stole the pot from the Ranch. "I enjoyed that," I said, "probably more than she will ever know." I stepped over to the bookcase and picked up the book containing *St. Mawr* and *The Man who Died*. "She can have this if she wants it. I've already read it."

"Thanks, Uncle Hubert. She loves to have books by and about Lawrence. Say, did that pot turn out to still be at the Ranch after all these years?"

"After all these years, I'm certain it's not there now. How's your financial situation?"

"Glad you asked. I had to give up one of my part-time jobs, and with the summer session tuition..."

He rambled on about his financial woes, and I listened lazily, happy the subject had been changed. Before he left, I gave him some money. It was more than I generally give him because I was confident the pots Cyril had brought were going to bring me a great deal of money.

54

Whit Fletcher came by the shop just before closing time the next day and brought me up to date on the day's developments. The scales of justice were settling back into balance.

As I walked across to *Dos Hermanas*, I spotted a young couple kissing on one of the benches in the plaza, and it put me in mind of a song, *The Old Lamp Lighter*. I'm familiar with three versions by Kay Kyser, Bing Crosby, and Sammy Kaye. One verse goes:

> If there were sweethearts in the park,
> He'd pass a lamp and leave it dark,

It was a little early for streetlights, and these days they work with some sort of sensor that knows when it's dark and turns them on automatically. The old lamplighter has been done in by technology. Oh well, he's not the first.

The next verse goes:

> For he recalls when dreams were new,
> He loved someone who loved him, too.

I can't say it was love. I know it wasn't a dream. Just a lovely evening on my patio that would now be nothing more than a memory. I whistled the tune as I walked along. I can't say I felt happy, but I wasn't sad either. Maybe pensive is the right word. At any rate, a smile came unbidden to my lips when I saw Susannah at our table. She had her thick brown hair gathered into dog ears, and she was holding aloft a salt-rimmed glass, so I knew she had ordered for me because she takes her margaritas without salt. That may be her only fault.

"Margarita and I have been waiting for you."

"Sorry I'm late. Whit came by to bring me up to date on what happened today."

"Before you tell me that, I have a lot of questions I've been dying to ask you."

I took a sip of the margarita and told her I was ready.

"O.K., first question. Why wasn't Maria there?"

"Let's talk about that later. What's the second question?"

She gave me an inquisitive glance. "O.K. If Rich, Winant, and Glain were all on the Gaming Commission, why didn't they know each other?"

"That one's easy. Remember they are *new* members. They were just appointed about a month ago and the Commission meets quarterly, so they had yet to attend their first meeting. Next question."

"Why couldn't the University contact all the donors when the event was cancelled?"

"I don't know. I know Carl Wron doesn't have voice mail and doesn't always answer his phone. I heard it ring while sitting on his porch and he made no move to answer it. Saunders is retired and doesn't keep a regular schedule. Betty lives alone and flits around a lot enjoying the money she inherited. I don't know about Glover. Maybe he was taking a customer for an extended test-drive."

"But why was Benthrop there after the event was cancelled? I can understand not reaching a few of the donors, but Benthrop works for the university. You would think they could get in touch with him at least."

"He teaches only two classes a week, seminars on Monday and Wednesday. By the time the decision was made to cancel, he had left town. Since professors aren't required to keep regular hours or report to their department heads, no one knew where he was. Turns out he went up to Taos early to do some shopping, and he drove up to the Ranch on Friday right before the snow started."

"O. K., here's the biggie – why did she do it?"

"Whit told me they found close to a hundred thousand dollars in cash hidden in her place in Taos. They traced the money back to an organization called the Consortium of New Mexico Entertainment Establishments which has the rather unfortunate acronym of CONMEE. Its only members are a few rogue casinos the State's been trying to shut down for years."

"How did the State allow them to be built in the first place?"

"When the State first approved Indian Gaming, a bunch of tribes just started building, and since they have a kind of sovereignty, no one paid much attention. But one of the casinos was built by a group that is not a recognized tribe and the legitimate tribes have joined the Gaming Commission's suit to shut it down. Another casino in CONMEE was originally granted a license by the Commission, but violated the law by hiring executives who had criminal records, and the Commission is also trying to shut them down."

"So maybe their acronym is appropriate."

"Exactly. But meanwhile, they pay their lawyers to delay and they rake in money."

"Enough to pay Adele Carlton a hundred thousand dollars?"

"You know how much gambling brings in, Suze? I think it was about eight hundred million last year."

"But how much of that was in New Mexico?"

"All of it. I'm just talking about New Mexico. That's over two million a day!"

"But surely even CONMEE doesn't hire hit-women."

"Whit says their official position is they paid Carlton as a lobbyist to influence the Gaming Commission."

"I guess killing off the members is one form of influence," she joked, and then she thought for a while and said, "You said Agatha Cruz's glasses were greasy. Or should I say Adele Carlton's glasses were greasy?"

"Agatha Cruz was a character being played by Adele, so I guess we can talk about Agatha just like we talk about other characters in a play or movie. And the greasy glasses? They helped me to figure it all out."

"How?"

"Well, it wasn't what started me wondering about Cruz, but once I did start wondering, it helped complete the picture. When I first saw her glasses, I just thought here's an old lady whose eyesight is so bad she doesn't even know her glasses need cleaning. But once I began to wonder if it was an act, I remembered a girl I knew at UNM who was majoring in rehabilitation."

"And I thought I knew all the majors."

"In one of her classes – the girl's name was Betsy – the teacher made them rub petroleum jelly on their glasses and walk around campus for a day so they would have more empathy for people with vision problems."

"Wouldn't people majoring in rehab have empathy to begin with?"

"You would hope so."

"And what about students who didn't wear glasses?"

"Maybe they gave them theatrical glasses, ones that just have plain glass. I saw some of those at the costume and theater shop."

"So how did cute little Betsy walking around with Vaseline on her glasses help you figure out that Agatha Cruz was a fake?"

"Cute little Betsy had an underslung jaw and one solid eyebrow that covered both eyes."

"That's called a unibrow."

"I didn't know that. Anyway, when she greased up her glasses, she moved slowly and tentatively to avoid tripping because she couldn't judge the height of curbs and thresholds, and she would reach out slowly because she couldn't tell how far away a door knob or a pencil on a desk was. The result was that she moved exactly like an elderly person."

"I don't think we say 'elderly' anymore, Hubie."

"O.K., she moved like a senior citizen, one with a bushy unibrow. Agatha put grease on her glasses to make her move like a senior citizen. That's a lot easier than faking the movements, even for an actress."

"But what first got you suspicious?"

"You get the credit, Suze. When I thought more about where Cruz had gone and the lack of tracks, and when I dismissed anyone coming up or down the cliff, I realized we had a locked-room mystery just like you said. And I remembered that you said one version was that the murderer was in the room all along but cleverly hidden."

"Being under a bed is not that clever, Hubert."

"I know that, but if there's an open window, who's going to look under the bed? Come to think of it, why would a murderer hide under the bed in the circumstances we were in anyway? The killer would have to come out eventually and couldn't get away without being seen. But if you can come out from under the bed *as a different person*, then you're home free. And you also get credit for the 'different person' idea because you explained that the character in *The Man Who Died* was both Isiris and Jesus. I also remembered in *And Then There Were None*, the judge says the murderer, 'could only come to the island in one way. It's perfectly clear. He is one of us'. That led me to the hypothesis that Agatha and Adele might be the same person. Then I thought about the wet robe and sneakers, the greasy glasses, and the smell, and it all fell into place."

"So Adele glued on fake wrinkles, put on a grey wig, and greased up her glasses."

"Right."

"What about Carrasco?"

"He was a cool customer. He knew his true identity wouldn't stay hidden, so when he drove down to get the police, he told them right off who he was and said he'd been filling in for a friend. Pretending to be someone else isn't a crime unless you do so for criminal purposes, and he more or less had Canon's permission anyway. You know something, Suze? I should have figured him out. The University blazer he was wearing didn't fit him. He didn't know about the electricity situation when we asked, and he didn't know how far it was to the main road when Saunders asked him."

"You think he was in on the murders?"

"He didn't do them, but it's hard to believe he didn't know what his girlfriend was up to. He certainly knew afterwards. The police let him go last night from my shop only because they wanted to follow him. He led them to a dumpster a few blocks from Srini's apartment. He dug around in it until he found an iron bar, and then the police grabbed him."

"The murder weapon!"

"Yep. He led them right to it."

"So he's an accessory."

"Yeah, but only after the fact, which is not as serious, and he was trying to help the woman he loves. Who knows if a jury would convict him. He could even claim he was trying to help the police find the murder weapon."

"I don't think that would fly, Hubie. So he may not go to jail?"

"Not unless she implicates him. But she hasn't so far, and how would that help her?"

"Maybe she'd get a lighter sentence?"

"I don't think it works that way. They lessen the sentences for small fish who rat out the big fish. They already have the big fish. My guess is she doesn't want to implicate him. She loves him and wants him to be waiting for her when she gets out."

"You don't think she'll get the death penalty?"

"This isn't Texas, Suze. There has been exactly one person executed in New Mexico in the last thirty years. Anyway, her lawyers will probably plead insanity."

"You think she's crazy, Hubert?"

"She's an actress, Suze. Maybe she can convince a jury."

"And she's pretty good, Hubie. It can't be that easy pretending to be another person for three days. I wonder if they have a theater group in the women's prison."

It was a pleasant spring evening with just a touch of smoke in the air from people burning their grass so their lawns would green up sooner. It's illegal now, but people still do it, and it still works.

We waved for Angie and got another round. After it came and we sampled the fresh chips, salsa, and drinks, Susannah sat back in her chair and asked me if I wanted to answer the first question now.

I said I did and told her Maria wasn't there because she told Whit she didn't want to come.

"I don't think Carrasco or Carlton wanted to come either, but he didn't give them a choice," she noted.

"Yeah. I guess Whit could have forced Maria to come as a material witness or something, and when he told me she had refused to attend, he did ask if I wanted him to force the issue, and I said no."

"You didn't want her there?"

"I didn't want to force her into an uncomfortable situation."

"You were afraid she'd take off her clothes again?"

I almost choked on my drink. After I stopped coughing, I told her the reason it would have been uncomfortable was that there was someone there other than me who Maria was sort of involved with romantically.

She gave me a puzzled look, and I sat back in my chair and watched her going through the list of attendees in her mind.

"One of the uniformed policemen?"

I shook my head.

"Fred Givens?"She sounded a little incredulous on that one.

"No."

"It can't be Carrasco. All the other guys are too old except... Oh my God! Don't tell me it's Srini."

"It isn't Srini."

"Whew. Surely not Tristan."

"Nope."

All that leaves is Figg, and surely she—"

"It's not Figg."

"But I've mentioned everyone who was there."

"You haven't mentioned Don Canon."

"I ruled him out because Maria would have recognized Carrasco was not Canon."

"She didn't know Canon."

"But you said they were romantically involved."

"I said sort of. They had recently been corresponding through a computer dating service."

"Where you don't give your last name," she said knowingly.

"Right. Remember Don said last night that he didn't want to stay at the Ranch after he found out the event had been cancelled? The reason is he was hoping to go into town and actually meet Maria for the first time in person. But she didn't know that, so she accepted the catering offer from Carrasco pretending to be Canon. The name Canon didn't mean anything to her and Don is fairly common, so she had no reason to be suspicious. Then last Friday, she showed up on my doorstep and we had a romantic evening—"

"Until I barged in."

I waved the air. "Don't worry about it. You had good reason. Anyway, she wasn't there when I got back. I talked to the real Canon early Sunday afternoon in preparation for the big meeting in my shop. That's when I told him I would be calling on him to speak and we discussed what he would say. He told me he already knew quite a bit about what had gone on up at the Ranch. I asked him if the police had filled him in, and he said not very much, but he said he had learned more because he spent most of Saturday with a woman who had been at the Ranch with us."

"And you asked him who it was, and he said Maria Salazar."

I nodded.

"What did you say, Hubie?"

I sighed. "I said she seemed like a nice young lady, and he said she was and that he was smitten with her and that they had another date on Monday."

"That's tonight. Geez, Hubie, you must feel awful. You want to get drunk and forget her?"

"Maybe a little drunk. But I don't want to forget her. The memory is bittersweet."

"You're a real romantic, Hubie."

"I can't help it."

"Maybe she still likes you."

"Maybe she never really did," I said morosely.

"Then why did she take off all her clothes for you?"

I smiled at her. "Maybe it was another case of paradoxical undressing."

55

I was sitting with Ninfa Sanchez under the pecan trees sipping fresh-squeezed limeade.

She has a long face, clear brown skin, and a hooked nose that makes her look like an Aztec carving. She's two or three inches taller than me and is too tall to be described as plump, so I guess maybe she's statuesque. Her long straight hair was pulled back severely and held with what looked like a piece of leather with a chopstick through it.

Emilio was in the house preparing lunch and had been firm in rejecting our offers to help. Consuela was still in the hospital.

"It's like being a little girl again," Ninfa said. Our homemade willow lawn chairs were next to each other but she was staring off towards the levee.

"Back in the house you grew up in."

"Not just that. He does everything for me. I can't cook, clean, run a wash. Hell, I should just stay here."

"Beto wouldn't like that."

"You might be surprised."

I decided not to pursue that remark. Consuela and Emilio were sad when Ninfa and Beto moved to California, but Beto had a good job offer and they settled into a small tract house in Orange County that's probably worth half a million now even though it's not in a particularly upscale neighborhood.

"You look good," I said.

"For someone who just had a body part removed?"

"That's one way to thin down."

She laughed and then told me her mother had two great hopes – to have a grandchild and to live close to her daughter. "I've withheld both from her," she said.

"There's plenty of time. My mother was forty one when I was born."

"Beto doesn't want children."

"You could move back here. One out of two ain't bad."

"Beto says he won't work for the slave wages they pay here."

"And your parents can't afford California."

"And wouldn't leave here even if they could afford it," she said and turned to look at me. "I guess it's a Mexican standoff."

I looked up into the trees. You're supposed to be able to tell how good the pecan crop will be by examining the spring foliage, but I don't know how to do that. It's sort of like telling how long it will rain, an interesting skill but one I have no need for. Of course I have no need to look at the heavens through my telescopes and I do that.

"I can't come back here, Hubert."

Ninfa had always been slightly rebellious. When I think back on her as a small child, I always picture her with her chin stuck out.

"You gave her part of you, Ninfa. You gave her life. You should feel good about that."

"It's not what she wanted."

"It's not what she *says* she wanted," I corrected.

"You think so?"

"It doesn't matter what you say. She thinks someday you'll have children."

"She thinks that's what women do."

"It *is* what women do. Most of them. It isn't *all* they do."

"What? You're a feminist philosopher now?"

Defiant. That's the word I was searching for. "You gave her more time. More time to hope."

"I'm not going to have children, Hubert."

I was still looking up at the pecan leaves. "She doesn't believe that."

"You think hope is enough?"

"It's better than no hope. And she'll be less frantic because death is not so imminent."

"Thanks to you," she said, still looking off in the distance.

"You're the one who gave her a kidney."

"You're the one who paid for it."

"It was paid—"

"And don't give me that bullshit about insurance. My parents believe you because they don't know any better. But what kind of health insurance can you get where the insured never filled out any forms, never signed anything? Still never sign anything. But you say they have insurance and they believe you."

"Belief is good, too," I said. "Like hope."

56

We were out on the veranda of *Dos Hermanas*, square in the rays of the setting sun. I used to worry about skin cancer, but a New Mexico evening is worth the risk.

"I was impressed with how you solved the murders at the Lawrence Ranch, Hubie."

"Thanks, Suze. I couldn't have done it without you. I'll bet you can solve another mystery."

"Which mystery?"

"The one of my missing pot."

"How could I do that?"

"By the oldest reasoning process known to man, the process of elimination."

"It's known to women too, Hubert. O.K., I guess my theory about someone coming in from outside the Conference Center was pretty much blown out of the water when we discovered Adele was the culprit."

I nodded.

"So it had to be one of the sixteen people there."

"Fifteen."

"Oh, right. Cruz wasn't a real person. I know it wasn't you or me. I'm just as sure it wasn't Srini. It obviously wasn't one of the three victims."

"See, you've eliminated six people already."

"I don't think any of the four donors would steal it. They're all rich and give to a good cause. Plus, they just seem like nice people."

"Now you're down to five suspects."

"I don't think it was Maria. I don't think it was Carrasco or Carlton. When you're sneaking around pretending to be someone else and killing people, you probably aren't thinking about lesser crimes like petty theft."

"An Anasazi pot is hardly petty."

"You know what I mean. So that leaves Vasquez and Benthrop. Vasquez is a little slick, but what do you expect? He's a lobbyist. But I don't see him as a thief, so it must be Benthrop. Was it Benthrop, Hubie? I really hope it was him."

"I don't know, but I went through the same process of elimination and came up with the same result. And I also remembered something. When we were in Fred Rich's room after he was killed, Benthrop was the first to leave, so he would have been alone briefly in the main room."

"That's right," she agreed.

"At first I thought he left because he was embarrassed by that 'I'm a doctor' remark, but then I realized he's not the sort of person to be embarrassed by anything."

"Too caught up in himself."

"Exactly."

"So Benthrop did steal your pot."

"Well, we can't be certain of that. For all we know, Robert Saunders is a kleptomaniac."

"So what do we do to prove it was Benthrop?"

"We talk to Whit Fletcher."

57

"Three murders and the reward is a measly five thousand. Can you believe that? That's what – less than two thousand for each stiff. After I split it with you, that's what?"

"Eight hundred and thirty-three dollars and thirty-three and a third cents for each murder," I told him.

"If you say so. I tell you, Hubert, they say crime don't pay, but solving crimes don't pay much better."

I had cancelled my standing engagement at five because I wasn't planning to drink anything. It was a little past nine in the evening, and Fletcher was drinking coffee that had been steeping since that morning. He sat the cup down on my counter and swallowed without even flinching. Meanwhile, I was doing some quick thinking, and when I had done it, I told him he could keep the whole five thousand.

His attempt to contain his excitement was palpable – an extra twenty five hundred is a substantial boost for a cop's pay.

"What's the catch?"

"No catch. I just need a couple of favors."

"I figured as much."

"Nothing you wouldn't do anyway, Whit. And it may bring you another collar."

Then I told him about my suspicions that Benthrop had stolen my pot, and he asked me if I owned the pot or if it was one I had stolen myself. I told him the pot was all mine, bought and paid for from Martin's uncle. You know that isn't true, but he didn't and, as you will see, one of Martin's uncle's pots did come into play.

Fletcher also told me that when they questioned Benthrop about his activities before, during, and after the fateful weekend, the shopping he had been doing in Taos was for Native American handicrafts. That didn't surprise me in light of his belief that the next level of human consciousness would bring peoples of color into their ascendancy, or the next ascendancy of peoples of color would bring human consciousness into its next level, or whatever his nutty theory was. What I really wondered was whether his shopping for Native American artifacts had included the use of a five-finger credit card to add my pot to his collection.

So after Whit left, I wrapped one of Martin's Uncle's pots in bubble wrap and drove the Bronco to a parking lot on the east side of the University. From there I walked to a low-slung adobe on Buena Vista, three blocks from the lot.

I had Tristan's cell phone with me. I stood across the street and dialed. I spoke a few words and hung up. A few minutes later Benthrop emerged and sped away. The coast is clear, I thought to myself, and then realized I don't really understand that common phrase. Does it mean the weather on the coast is good? Does it mean there's no one guarding the coast so an amphibious assault will succeed? And why do I care? There are no coasts in the desert.

Then I shook myself out of this pointless woolgathering and set about the task at hand. I had brought along several thin pieces of plastic from among a collection of samples I obtained from an art supply store. I'm really not a burglar, but being able to loid a lock (open it by sliding a flexible strip of something between the spring-loaded bolt and the jamb; you've probably heard of this being done with credit cards) is sometimes useful. I didn't need to do it in this case because Benthrop had left in such a hurry that he didn't even bother to lock up.

I found my Anasazi pot after a few minutes of searching and I left the pot I had brought along in a different spot, one where Benthrop would be unlikely to look. Martin's uncle does excellent and complete glazing of all his pots, so being submerged in water would cause the pot no harm.

Susannah loves Bernie Rhodenbarr, a fictional burglar who steals not just for the money but also for the thrill. He loves to walk around the place he is burgling, read a book, even take a nap.

I prefer digging in the desert to breaking into houses. On the few occasions I've needed to break into a house, I get in and out as quickly as possible. And shake from my pounding heart in between.

But I knew Benthrop wasn't coming back anytime soon. A little voice suggested I take a look around. Maybe I had a hunch they would be there.

58

"So it was Benthrop. I'm glad it was him, Hubie."

"Because it shows the process of elimination works?"

"No, because he's an insect."

"I have to admit I enjoyed seeing him running away after Fletcher called him and said Carlton had escaped and was seen near his house."

"Couldn't Whit get in trouble for that?"

"He'll just deny he said it. Who's going to believe Benthrop over a detective on the Albuquerque Police Department?"

"So how did Benthrop look?' she asked gleefully.

"Even in the dark, you could see the whites of his eyes. He was terrified."

Now I remember. That's what *schadenfreude* means. We were on the veranda, drinks in hand, chips and salsa at the ready, and I was ogling the angular yet graceful Angie. I didn't need another round. I was just enjoying the sight of a sultry woman.

"There's one thing I don't understand, Hubie. Why did you hide one of Martin's uncle's pots? Couldn't the police have just gone in themselves and found the Anasazi pot like you did? Then you wouldn't have had to take the risk of breaking in."

"I didn't break in. The door was unlocked. But I had to switch the pots before the police went in. It wouldn't have worked if they had found the Anasazi pot. They need two things to charge him with theft. First they have to find the stolen item in his possession. Second, they have to prove it belongs to someone else. I can't prove the Anasazi pot is mine."

"But you found it yourself and dug it out of bat shit."

"I prefer to think of it as guano. Yeah, I found it, but it was illegal to dig it up."

"Then why do you display it right out in the open in your shop?"

"Because for all anyone knows, I dug it up before the passage of ARPA when treasure hunting was legal, and that's enough to satisfy a collector. But if Benthrop is charged with stealing it, his lawyer would no doubt want me to *prove* when I dug it up, and I can't do that."

"You didn't tell me where you hid the pot when you got inside Benthrop's house."

I started to say I hid the pot in the pot, but that's too much of a groaner even for me, so I told her I hid it in the toilet.

"Oh, yuk. Why did you do that, Hubert?"

"Not in the bowl, Suze, in the tank."

I sat back and pictured Benthrop's jaw hanging open as the police, warrant in hand, fished out the pot.

"So what do you think will happen to him?" she asked.

"I'm guessing five to ten years."

"For stealing one pot?"

I smiled at her. "That wasn't all he stole. For some reason I can't explain, I decided to look around his place."

"Wow, just like Bernie Rhodenbarr."

"Yeah, I thought about him. Guess what I found?"

"Something to steal?"

"Something already stolen – *War Shirt 1992*."

"He stole the paintings from the Church?"

"Either that or bought them from someone who did."

"That's great news for Jaune Quick-To-See Smith. She gets her paintings back and you get your pot back. But did you really have to give Fletcher your half of the reward to do that?"

"Maybe not. But I got a hundred thousand for the two Dulcinea pots, so I was feeling generous, and it doesn't hurt to have Whit thinking he owes me."

"How much did you have to spend on the medical bills?"

"About forty-seven thousand."

"God, that's expensive. Still, you cleared over fifty thousand. You're buying, right?"

"I'm buying, but I already spent some of the fifty."

"What did you do this time?"

"I set up three scholarships at the University."

She smiled. "For Rich, Winant, and Glain."

"Yeah, but only for ten thousand each, so I still cleared over twenty thousand, and tourist season is about to start, and I've got a lot of replicas ready, so things look pretty good."

"Of course things didn't quite work out between you and Maria, but there's always Betty."

"I don't think so, Suze. I called her, and she said she's seeing Carl Wron."

"Oh."

"Maria went for the younger man, Betty went for the older man, and I ended up being Mister In-Between. I guess they remembered that old Johnny Mercer song that tells us to accentuate the positive, eliminate the negative, and don't mess with Mister In-Between."

"Sorry, Hubie. But you still have Dolly."

I sighed. "She broke up with me the day we left for Taos."

"Why didn't you tell me? We were alone in the Bronco for hours."

"Well, the reason she gave at first was something I was hesitant to mention to you."

"We're best friends, Hubie. You can tell me anything." Then she got that crooked enigmatic smile and said, "Was it because you couldn't—"

"I never told you that!"

"So I guessed it. That *was* the reason."

"No it wasn't."

"Then what was it?"

"She said it was because I was taking you to Taos as my girlfriend."

"What? She knows we're just friends."

"Then she changed the reason and said it was because I stole her dog."

"You have *got* to be making this up."

I shook my head and took a sip of my drink. "Do you remember the saga of Dolly and Geronimo?"

She rolled her eyes. "You were trying to figure out which house on that street had some pots, and the best ruse you could come up with was to go door to door with Geronimo pretending to be a volunteer from the animal shelter looking for the owner of a lost dog. That was bizarre even by your standards."

"I prefer to think of it as ingenious. And it worked. I located the right house."

"But not before a murder had taken place in it for which you got blamed."

"And subsequently exonerated. No, Suze, it was a great plan. The only flaw was that Dolly volunteered to adopt Geronimo if the true owner couldn't be found."

"And when you kept him, you had to say that you had adopted him. Your whole relationship with Dolly has been built on a lie."

"That may be a bit strong. But she must have somehow figured out what happened."

"You think that's why she's been so unstable lately?"

I turned up my palms. "It's a mystery to me. I'm on the outs with Dolly, Betty, and Maria. Let's talk about you instead. You and Srini to be precise."

She leaned back in her chair and sighed. "You were right about how things work in India, at least in his case. He said he plans to go back there in August because his family has selected a bride for him."

Oops. Why did I have to bring this up? "But I thought you two had a date the other night."

"*I* thought it was a date. *He* thought we were just two friends having fun."

"So where does that leave us, Suze?"

"Back where we always are, Hubie. No romance in sight."

Somehow I thought she was mistaken, but that's probably just because I'm an optimist.

TURN THE PAGE FOR A SNEAK PREVIEW OF THE NEXT
POT THIEF ADVENTURE

The Pot Thief Who Studied Lew Wallace

"I would rather write another book than be rich." - Lew Wallace

I was on a ledge three hundred feet above the Rio Doloroso violating two federal laws, one on purpose and the other by accident.

I felt a little like Indiana Jones except for the fact that I was afraid to approach the precipice. But my acrophobia didn't stop me from digging. I'd been told there were ancient pots here, and I knew they would be in the ruins, not out on the ledge.

I'm not a professional archaeologist and I didn't have a permit to excavate, so I was violating the Archaeological Resources Protection Act (ARPA).

So what?

Because of the American Bar Association and the American Institute of Architects, it would be impossible today for Abe Lincoln to be a lawyer or Frank Lloyd Wright to be an architect.

And thanks to the Archaeological Institute of America, it's also impossible for me to hunt for artifacts legally. Which was why I was digging under the cover of darkness.

Every association of 'professionals' wants to exclude amateurs. And the club of millionaires called Congress caved in to the wishes of professional archaeologists and passed ARPA.

My name is Hubert Schuze, and I'm a treasure hunter. ARPA redefined me as a pot thief, but it was passed by the same legislature that approved a health care program with a price tag of 940 billion dollars and labeled it the 'Affordable Health Care Act'.

Here's a message for my representatives in Washington: Health care is not affordable and archaeological resources do not need protecting.

If they're resources, we should exploit them. That's what I do, and I'm positive that's what the people who created them would want.

I'm a potter myself, and after I'm long dead, I don't want the pots I made to be mouldering in the ground like John Brown's body. I want some enterprising lad like myself to dig them up, appreciate them, and make a few bucks in the process. Maybe he can earn enough to see a doctor.

I do feel bad about the second law I was breaking, the Native American Graves Protection and Repatriation Act (NAGPRA). Who other than a ghoul would violate that one?

But it wasn't my fault. I was digging in a ruin of residences. Prehistoric tribes didn't bury their dead in their living quarters. So you can imagine my surprise when I stuck my hand into the hole I'd dug and grasped another hand. I'd been hoping for an artifact, not a handshake.

It gets worse.

One of the tools I use is a piece of rebar. Knowing this would make professional archaeologists bite the bristles off their tiny brushes. But the success rate is low in treasure hunting. I can't afford to waste time digging in dry holes. So I use the rebar to probe through soft soil to discover whether there is anything solid below the surface.

When I feel the slightest resistance, I set the rebar aside and dig with my hands. I don't want to damage any potential merchandise. Usually what I find is a rock, root or piece of modern debris.

But in this case, the object impeding my rebar's advance through the soil was a human hand. I had accidentally desecrated human remains.

I felt woozy. The *chorizo* I'd wolfed down for energy gurgled up my esophagus. I swallowed hard to keep it down.

Then I heard an even louder gurgling. It wasn't my tummy rumbling. It was the familiar rurrer-rurrer-rurrer of the starter motor on my Bronco. Most people don't know what a starter motor sounds like. They turn the key and hear only the reassuring roar of the engine coming to life. They have shiny new cars. But a thirty-two-year-old Ford Bronco doesn't jump to life. Like its forty-something-year-old owner, it takes more time getting started than it used to.

I had left Geronimo in the Bronco. And while he sometimes displays a certain canine cunning, I didn't think he was capable of starting the thing. But couldn't he at least have barked at the car thief?

It wasn't that I minded losing the vehicle. But the rope that had lowered me down to the ruin – and by which I planned to ascend back to the surface – was attached to the winch.

I was stranded in a prehistoric cliff dwelling three hundred feet above the ground below and thirty feet below the ground above.

Thirty feet is not that far. If it isn't too steep, you could just walk up it. But then your enemies could come down it just as easily, which would defeat the purpose of a cliff dwelling.

Even if it were a perfectly vertical cliff, you could perhaps work your way up by using little rock fissures as hand and toe holds. But when the cliff is *past* vertical, when it slants away from the direction you want to go, the only way up is by rope. Like the one I had just watched disappear.

Of course there was another way out. There would be a path along the precipice to a point where the terrain allowed a narrow switchback climb up to the surface. Ancient cliff dwellers sought places with an overhang for protection and a narrow entrance path that could be easily guarded. One man can hold off an entire army if they have to approach single file. He just stands behind a big rock next to the narrowest part of the path and pushes them over the edge as they creep along.

Just the thought of that narrowest part of the path made me break out in a cold sweat.

2

Unless I wanted to spend the rest of my life in a cliff dwelling, I had to find that path and follow it.

But I wasn't going to risk it at night. And I wasn't going to sleep next to a disturbed grave. So I filled the hole and gently packed down the soil. I don't know any prayers for reinterment, but I said what came to mind and meant every word of it.

I had my first aid kit, water, matches, a flashlight and a warm jacket with a pocket full of *chorizo*. It wasn't everything you'd take on a wilderness camping trip, but it was enough. I also had a large gunny sack. I didn't get to carry a pot or two home in it as I had hoped, but it did come in handy in several ways. My final piece of equipment was the rebar, one end of which had recently poked a human hand.

I thought about tossing it over the ledge into the Rio Doloroso. But the way my luck was running, it would probably impale some wilderness trekker asleep in his tent. I didn't need that on my conscience, so I just stuck the thing in the ground, evil end first.

I rolled the jacket up for a pillow and bedded down behind what remained of a rock and mud wall. Maybe the prayer had cleansed my mind because I dropped off to sleep almost immediately.

The first time I woke up, it was because of the cold. I put the jacket on. The gunny sack was not substantial enough to make a pillow, but at least it saved me from having to sleep with my head directly on the ground.

The second time I woke up, it was because of the rustling sound.

There was no wind. Something was moving through the brush. And getting nearer. I pulled the rebar out of the ground. Let it be a skunk, I thought, although it was making way too much noise to be one.

A skunk would be okay. Even a bobcat. They seldom attach humans. Just not a mountain lion. Or worse, a badger. A badger would probably bite through the rebar before bulldozing me off the cliff.

It was just a few feet away. I could hear it panting. I raised the rebar above my head just as it broke into the clearing and lept at me.

It would've served him right if I'd brained him with the piece of iron. He didn't bark to scare away the car thief, and he didn't bark to let me know he was approaching. I swear he's part anteater. I don't think they bark. It would also explain the long neck that sags down and sways to and fro as he walks.

Despite the start he gave me, I was glad to see him. His feathery wagging tail and big sad eyes were part of it. But the main reason was that his arrival confirmed the path was still there and passable. He may be part anteater, but he is certainly not part mountain goat. If he could make it down the path, I could make it back up.

He inhaled the *chorizo* I gave him then started digging at the soft dirt I had tamped down. My explanation about the Native American Graves Protection and Repatriation Act fell on deaf ears (can anteaters hear?), so I piled the biggest rocks I could find on top of the grave.

I guess I've seen too many old westerns because the sight of the rock pile put me in mind to make a crude cross from two limbs and stick it between the stones. Then it occurred to me that someone born here four or five hundred years before Columbus was unlikely to have been a Christian.

I fell asleep thinking about what object or symbol might be appropriate for the grave.

And awoke for the third time to the sound of another critter coming down the trail. I have only one dog, so the same thoughts as before ran through my head except for the bear my overwrought imagination added to the mountain lion and the badger.

It was noisy and moving slowly. And dragging a chain.

A chain? On a cliff over the Rio Doloroso fifty miles from the nearest human habitation?

I tried to imagine what it could be. The ghost of grave robbers past? The angry spirit of the corpse I had impaled?

Geronimo whined and scooted back against the cliff. I joined him. For all I know, I was also whining. I was giving serious consideration to taking a running leap into the Rio Doloroso.

I figured there were two possibilities. The river would be dry, as it frequently is, and I would go splat on its rocky bed. Or I might land in water deep enough to survive the fall. Since I can't swim, I would drown. Both options seemed preferable to being eaten alive by a bear or mountain lion. And what more appropriate place to die than one named *doloroso*?

But it was neither a bear nor a mountain line. It was a young coyote dragging a chain attached to a trap clamped on his left front foot. There was a lot of blood on his leg and quite a bit on his muzzle.

The stories of coyotes chewing off a foot to escape a trap are pure myth. He had licked the wound because it hurt, not to attempt self-amputation. How he managed to pull the stake out of the ground I don't know. Maybe the idiot who set the trap didn't anchor it properly.

I tossed a *chorizo* to him. He sniffed at then ate it.

He looked down at his leg then up at me. It's tempting to say he wanted help, but I don't believe coyotes see humans as helpers. The Wildlife Service kills over six thousand coyotes in New Mexico every year by trapping, snaring, shooting, poisoning, and aerial gunning.

Yes, aerial gunning. They shoot them from helicopters and small planes. Keep that in mind the next time you see one of those highway signs that read, "speeding enforced by aircraft."

One moment you're motoring down the interstate. The next you're taken out by an air-to-surface missile.

About the Pot Thief Series

The Pot Thief Who Studied Pythagoras, The Pot Thief Who Studied Ptolemy, The Pot Thief Who Studied Einstein, and The Pot Thief Who Studied Escoffier are available in paperback from your local independent bookseller, Barnes & Noble, Amazon and the publisher, Aakenbaaken & Kent. Signed copies are sometimes available from the many bookstores where the author has done signings. They are also available directly from the author: ThePotThief@gmail.com. E-book versions of all *Pot Thief* books are available from Amazon.com.

CPSIA information can be obtained at www.ICGtesting.com
Printed in the USA
LVOW060457050712

288808LV00003B/1/P